BOOKS BY DARA GIRARD

Duvall Sisters

The Glass Slipper Project

Taming Mariella

A Reluctant Hero

The Black Stockings Society

Power Play

A Gentleman's Offer

Body Chemistry

Round the Clock

Return of the Black Stockings Society

Playing for Keeps

After Hours

A Private Affair

Just One Look

Private Lessons

The Main Attraction

Ladies of the Pen

Words of Seduction

Pages of Passion

Beneath the Covers

Henson Series

Table for Two

Gaining Interest

Careless Rapture

Dangerous Curves

Familiar Stranger

It Happened One Wedding

Unexpected Pleasure

Midnight Promise

Sweet Temptation

Always and Forever

Truly Yours

Say Yes

Picture Perfect

Clifton Sisters

The Sapphire Pendant

The Amber Stone

The Emerald Ring

Fortune Brothers

A Tempting Proposal

A Seductive Arrangement

An Unforgettable Moment

Novels

Honest Betrayal

PLAYING FOR KEEPS

DARA GIRARD

Λ

ISBN: 978-1949764529

PLAYING FOR KEEPS

ILORI PRESS BOOKS, LLC

P.O. Box 10332

Silver Spring, MD 20914

www.iloripressbooks.com

CHAPTER ONE

SHE SHOULDN'T HAVE USED a sledgehammer, Stacy Price thought as she heard the jail bars close behind her. Yes, the sledgehammer had definitely been a mistake. But it had just been sitting there and looked so tempting. She suppressed a smile. It had also felt good, but now she had to face the consequences. Iron bars, cold, concrete walls and uniformed guards. All because she'd lost. Not her mind, although some thought she had, but her sense of dignity. Her integrity. If she hadn't lost, she wouldn't be here, with nothing else to do but notice every shade of gray that surrounded her.

He'd won. The lazy, no good bastard had won. She hadn't expected that and she usually expected everything. Stacy prided herself on being prepared for any outcome. But that Thursday afternoon she'd sat in divorce court unable to look at her lawyer. She couldn't see anything--rage blinded her. She could understand why bulls were triggered by the color red because for a second that's all she saw. Red--blood red. Her ex was entitled to alimony plus half of all the royalties from her published books. She took a moment to glance at his smug handsome face and briefly thought it would be worth twenty-five to life to get rid of it permanently. She'd supported him and his failed artistic endeavors for ten years and now she had to pay him?

She couldn't believe he'd been able to convince the judge that he'd been instrumental in her success. Success she'd worked hard for. She'd endured years of rejections, bad contracts and lonely nights until the right book--her fourth--took off. If only she could kill him off in a book, that would be cathartic, but she hadn't been able to write in months. Actually, in years, if she was completely honest. She'd gotten away with writing essays, but nothing fictional. And the joy she'd once had when she wrote was gone. She wasn't sure she would ever be able to freely write again. And now she had to pay him until he remarried, but she knew he never would. There was no incentive. She knew he'd just shack up with some lady friend instead, and they could both live off of what she had been ordered to pay him monthly. She'd been thrown to the wolves.

"We can fight this," her lawyer said. He was a tall, balding man with a limp mustache who liked wearing expensive shoes. But his tone already sounded defeatist. It had always been that way, despite the large amount of money she paid him. She'd innocently thought at least the money would motivate some enthusiasm, but it never did. He'd told her things would be difficult from the get go. "Marshall is very likable," her lawyer had said with a tired sigh, while insinuating she should raise the white flag of surrender. "And you're well...competent."

"And that's a bad thing?" Stacy asked.

He sighed again, this time pinching the bridge of his nose, as though he were trying to fend off an oncoming headache. "Yes. You're an attractive, rich, successful woman. You won't garner the same level of sympathy he will. He's charming."

Of course her lawyer didn't need to tell her that. She already knew it. She'd fallen for his charm. Marshall was always charming. Sinfully so and he'd just sent her to hell.

That day in the courtroom, after she heard the judgment, Stacy remained silent as her lawyer packed up his things. She didn't reply to his offhanded comment, about his regrets, afraid that if she spoke fire would come out of her mouth. She hadn't felt such rage since--she couldn't remember when. She didn't want to talk to anyone. She stormed out of the building hoping the cool spring breeze would help. It didn't. Spring in New York was beautiful, there had been songs written about it, but at that moment, she couldn't give a damn. The bright sun blinded her and the sound of chirping birds annoyed her. What right did they have to be so happy? Then she saw a young couple holding hands, the man bending over and stealing a kissing, and the woman laughing in return. Love. How could love turn so sour? She noticed a crew of construction workers in hard hats glance at a woman passing by. The woman deserved their look. She was attractive, stylish and young, wearing a free flowing red skirt and matching killer high heels. Stacy looked at her with envy. She'd once been like that, but Marshall had taken that carefree confidence from her. She now felt old and used up at thirty-four.

She marched down the court steps and through the parking lot. That's when she saw it. Marshall's beautiful black BMW. The one she'd bought for him. The one she'd hope would make him stop being jealous of her career. The one she hoped would give him confidence. She was always trying to build up his esteem. His damn self-esteem. It wasn't until it was too late that she realized he was crushing hers. Stacy walked over to the car, took her car keys out of her handbag and carved her name in the door then used her lipstick to write a foul word on his window. But it didn't seem like enough. It was too simple. She wanted to send a stronger message.

Then she saw something out of the corner of her eyes: A sledgehammer. It had been left, by one of the workers, leaning up against a tree. She still didn't remember picking it up. What happened next was all a blur, rage making her strong, despair making her blind. She swung at the car and instantly heard glass shattering, another swing and she heard the sound of crushing metal. Then screams of horror and surprise blended with the sound of her destruction. She didn't care. She wanted the black car destroyed, just like he'd destroyed her life, her heart. She swung again and again and again, hot tears sliding down her face, sweat gliding down her forehead.

"I think you missed a spot," a deep voice said from behind her.

Stacy spun around ready to face her ex-husband, eager to tell him where he could shove his suggestion. She looked up, then froze, with her mouth open and her eyes wide. Marshall wasn't standing there, another man was. A handsome man with a face that was vaguely familiar. He had beautiful, laughing dark brown eyes that pierced her to the very core, as if he could see all her pain. And in an instant, he made her feel okay, made her feel that she mattered when just moments ago she felt as if she didn't. She could tell he was really looking at her--as if she were the only person there. And for one wild, brief moment she wanted to pour her heart out to him, to tell him of her dreams, hopes and fears, but of course she didn't. He was a stranger, no matter how visceral her attraction was to him. Her attraction to him shocked her, because she never thought she'd respond in such a primal way to a man again.

He was dressed casually in jeans, a jacket and baseball cap and hadn't shaved in a few days, which gave him a rugged appearance she didn't mind. He also had an oddly amused expression that puzzled her. Stacy wiped a trail of sweat from her forehead with the back of her hand. She blinked quickly, trying to see him clearly through her tears. "What?"

"I said you missed a spot." He pointed to the back of the car. "That section still looks brand new."

He was right. She hadn't even gotten to that section yet. She walked over to that area and gave it a hard whack. Again, feeling better after the effort. "Thanks."

"No problem," he said in a cool, conversational tone. "When you're done, could you tell me what you have against my car?"

Stacy turned sharply to him. "Your what?"

"My car."

She looked at the car then back at him. "*This* is your car?"

He nodded.

She licked her lips and took a deep breath hoping he was wrong. "Are you sure?"

He nodded again, but his dark brown eyes still appeared amused.

Stacy felt her stomach drop to her feet. "No, but that can't be. I bought this car. I know this car. I--" She let her gaze drop to the license plate then swore. Oh, no. She should have looked at it first. Oh god! She'd smashed the wrong car! She squeezed her eyes shut, wishing she could disappear. But she didn't. She took a deep breath and slowly turned and faced the man. She set the sledge-hammer down and kept her voice calm. "There's been a mistake. I am so very sorry. I can't even begin to tell you. You must be furious."

He folded his arms, not in an aggressive manner, but in a distant observant way as if he were at an art exhibition. "No, just stunned. I've never seen a woman work a sledgehammer like that. I'm sure the fury will come later."

Stacy couldn't understand why he was taking everything so well, but didn't want his good mood to end. She frantically dug into her purse for her cell phone. "Let's exchange information and I'll pay for the damages. What's your name?"

His brows shot up. "Really? You don't know who I am?"

Her head shot up and she blinked at him, trying to place him. Damn. Should she know him? Was he some foreign dignitary? A mayor? A celebrity? She hadn't kept up with the media lately. "Of course I do," she said trying to cover up her blunder. "I'm just not good with names."

His eyes twinkled. "You really don't know who I am, do you?"

She bit her lip."Well, you do look familiar."

"Yes, I have that kind of face." He noticed someone taking photos with their camera. He kept his back to them and his ball cap down low. He took out his cell phone. "Listen, before this gets ugly, just give me your number and--"

Without warning, a booming male voice cut through his words. "There she is! Arrest her!"

The stranger in front of her swore and Stacy shifted her gaze to another man--clean cut and enraged--coming towards them with two police officers by his side.

"Lady, put your hands up," one officer said, holding a gun on her.

Stacy shook her head. "Wait, please--"

"Hands up! Don't make us ask again."

The stranger turned. "Officers."

The office kept the gun aimed on Stacy. "Sir, please stand aside. Lady, put your hands behind your head."

Stacy did. One officer, a female, spun her around to face the car. "Do you have any other weapons on you?" the officer asked as she patted Stacy down.

"No."

"You're under arrest for vandalism," she said taking one of Stacy's hands and placing it in handcuffs and reading Stacy her Miranda Rights."

"No, wait. I didn't--"

"Ma'am, please stay calm. You can say your piece down at the station."

The owner of the car stepped forward. "Officers, there's no need to do this."

"Chance, leave this to me," the other man said. "It's my job to keep you safe. Thank you officers."

Stacy kept her head low. Within minutes she was shackled in handcuffs and sitting in the back of a squad car.

∾

"WHAT THE HELL WERE YOU THINKING?" her friend Julia Jacobs said as she drove Stacy home. Julia was a successful stage and film producer with enviable skill, who looked the part. If she were to run an ad it would read 'You'll never be rich enough to look this good', but Julia, who was Stacy's best friend and confidante, was more friendly and down-to-earth than her appearance gave her credit for.

"I wasn't thinking at all," Stacy said in a dull tone.

"Of all the people I thought I'd have to bail out of jail I never pictured you. I shouldn't have listened to you and gone with you to court. I take it things didn't go well?"

"Worse."

"I'm sorry Stacy, but you can't just vandalize cars because you're upset. You're facing felony charges."

"I know."

"I've already contacted your lawyer. You're going to plead not guilty."

"But I am guilty."

Julia sent her a quick, hard look. "Didn't you just hear what I said? You're facing felony charges, that puts prison time on the table. Do you want that?"

"I don't know if I care right now," Stacy said rubbing her eyes, wondering why crying made them feel so dry.

"Stacy. Let me handle things."

"Can't you just call the guy and tell him I'll buy him a new car?"

"That's the second part," Julia said with renewed energy. "You really know how to screw up big. He's a known director and producer. Of all the cars in the parking lot to whack, you had to choose Tyson Engel's."

"Tyson who?"

"Have you been living under a rock?"

"Yes," Stacy said, making no denial of her hermit like existence. After having to deal with Marshall and the courts for the past three years, she rarely looked at the TV, online chatter or the news. She just stayed to herself, eager to let the world pass by without her.

"He works with that actor C--"

Stacy held up her hand and shook her hand. "I really don't care. I'd hoped we could have settled this outside of court. I thought since he was unshaven and ragged looking that he'd go for financial compensation, but I was wrong."

"Tyson is clean shaven. Who are you talking about?"

"The other guy."

"What other guy?"

"There was another guy. He said the car was his."

"Never mind, we'll get this all sorted out. At least

your divorce is finally over. Marshall is out of your life and you can start fresh."

"He's not out of my life." Stacy gripped her hands into fists. "I'll be reminded of him every month when I have to pay--"

Julia lightly patted one of Stacy's clenched fists. "You can't let bitterness over take you."

"I wish I knew how to stop it." It seemed to cling to her. She envied couples every time she saw them. Their united joy amazed her. Had she really felt like that once? Would she ever feel like that again? She doubted it. Love had burned her too deeply. She wouldn't trust another man again.

"You don't mean that," Julia said.

"Don't mean what?"

"That you'll never love again."

Stacy sneered and looked at her friend. "I hate when you do that." They were close enough to sense each other's moods and at times, guess each other's thoughts. "I wish I'd never met him."

"He did force you to start writing."

"Are you going to give him credit for my career too?"

"Stop it. I'm on your side, I'm just saying there's no use wishing for something that won't change. Something you can't change."

"I know."

"The right man is out there for you."

Stacy shook her head. "No, I'm through with men. The only men I'll get close to are the ones in my dreams." She sighed. "I can't believe I'm ending up back in court again. God, my life is starting to sound like a tragic country-western song."

And Stacy still felt that way as she walked down the long jail corridor with sounds of shouts and bars opening and closing filling the air. She'd been forced to enter a plea deal, and ordered to teach creative writing to inmates and enroll in an anger management class. Funny thing was, she didn't want to manage her anger, she wanted it to go away.

CHAPTER TWO

STACY PRICE. After all these years. She didn't recognize him, but he hadn't forgotten her. Chance shook his head and softly swore. He knew he never would, even though he'd tried.

"What's that face for?"

"What face?" Chance said in a bored tone.

"You look unhappy."

"I still don't think we should have--"

"You're still thinking about the court case?" Tyson Engels said, stunned. "That's over. Hell, I still feel bad about the whole thing. I had you come to the court to be a character witness in my divorce and you end up getting attacked by a lunatic."

"She wasn't a lunatic."

Tyson shivered. "And I thought my ex was scary." He pointed at Chance. "Let this be a lesson to you. Don't get married."

Chance got up and went over to look out the window

of Tyson's Manhattan office. He gazed down at the yellow cabs making their way through the clogged traffic, then lifted his gaze to the high-rises in the distance. At times his life still felt like a dream. That he had a successful career and business still amazed him. But marriage somehow continued to be out of reach, although he had many opportunities. Unfortunately, he had too many secrets to let anyone close, although many women had tried. Seeing Stacy again made him realize how alone he felt. "I told you I wanted to drop the case," he said without turning around.

"You would have let her walk."

Yes, he would have let her get away with anything if he had the power, just so he could have the chance to be with her again. "I would have at least talked to her. Not given her a record."

"She's dangerous. She was wielding a sledgehammer. Plus, did you even notice how many people were taking pictures and videos?"

"No."

"Exactly, because you don't think about things like your image."

"I do. I was going to get her information and settle things." He would have gotten her phone number and made sure she didn't forget who he was this time.

"Do you know what your problem is?"

Chance started to grin, despite his annoyance. That phrase was one his friend's favorites. "I bet you're going to tell me."

"You're too nice. I mean how much did you get for that bit part in the indie movie you just finished?"

"I didn't do it for the money. The script was great and I got to work with actors who I respect."

"Actors whose names are already bigger than yours. How do you expect to stand out?"

"I don't." He knew that Tyson didn't understand. Chance loved to act and working with masters of the craft had been an exhilarating experience for him. Sure, his role in his last film had been small, but it had been a way for him to learn and grow. He'd started his own production company with Tyson so that he could do indie productions and keep his life interesting, plus have another income stream while he also helped other artists. He'd been fortunate enough to have a regular role on a hit TV show so he didn't have to scramble for different roles.

"Listen, you have the looks of a movie star, you don't want to end up as just a character actor. You have to be more strategic about the roles you take. Shave the beard and be the man women swoon over."

Chance absently rubbed his beard. "I'm shaving it soon. I have to be on the set in a few weeks. It will be gone by then." He sighed. Maybe the beard had been the reason why she hadn't recognized him. And, it had been more than ten years ago. Besides, he wasn't the gangly man in his early twenties anymore. He wondered what had happened to her. What had made her so upset? He hated that his friend had added to her misery by refusing to drop the charges no matter how right and logical it seemed.

Tyson rolled his eyes reading the expression on Chance's face. "Forget about her."

Chance sent him a look. "It's not that easy."

"It's not like she's a real looker anyway."

"She used to be."

"What?"

Chance silently swore annoyed by his slip. "Nothing. I'm just saying maybe she used to be."

"Maybe," Tyson allowed but sounded doubtful.

Chance gritted his teeth hating the tone of disbelief in his friend's words. He knew that Stacy hadn't always looked so unremarkable and average. She'd once brightened a room with her laughter, her brown sparkling eyes always making him feel she knew something about life he didn't and he'd wanted her to teach him. Back then, her chestnut skin was always draped in colorful scarves and she loved wearing an array of artistic jewelry. She'd had an arresting beauty--now it was faded. He'd seen an angry, defeated figure that broke his heart. He heard Tyson say something, but his friend's words merely sounded like a buzz in his ears. "What?"

"I said she could have been a stalker."

Chance returned his gaze to the window watching a bicycle messenger, with a bright red helmet, zip through traffic. "She didn't even recognize me."

"She was lying."

"She wasn't lying. Trust me, contrary to what you think, not everyone knows who I am."

"Enough do. Important people. Fortunately, I could take action because it was my car."

"You sold it to me." Chance turned from the window, his look hard.

Tyson held up his hands in a semi act of surrender. "Yes, yes, I know, but we hadn't made it official yet, so I could file the complaint. Forget about her. Let me handle things. It could be useful in the future."

The future. Right now thinking of Stacy didn't make him think of the future. Just his past and how far he'd come. Back to a time when he'd meet someone who didn't fawn over him. Someone who treated him like a regular guy. But it was all out of his hands now. Stacy wouldn't want to see him again as Chance Jamison and she didn't remember the man he used to be. And if she wanted to forget the past he'd let her. But could he?

∽

HELL HAD A SMELL--STALE COFFEE, cheap perfume and body odor. Stacy looked at the female guard and counted to ten. The woman's hair was in an intricate array of corkscrew curls, at least three different colors, and she had glitter on the tips of her eyelashes. The eyelashes didn't soften her look and Stacy thought they looked more appropriate for someone attending an underground party than in an office setting. Stacy reminded herself that she wouldn't--couldn't--get angry. She wouldn't let the other woman's attitude upset her. Anger had gotten her here in the first place and, if she wasn't careful, she'd end up there for good. Besides, the woman probably had had a bad day. Stacy wished she could summon up the emotion to care. It was her first day at the women's detention center and things were not going well. To begin with, when she had turned up at the facility, the staff up front gave her a hard time and told her that her name was not on the list.

"I am the instructor for the women's creative writing class," she'd said.

"Sorry, but we don't have you on our list."

"Listen, I was ordered to teach this class and it is supposed to start today." The guard looked her up and down, then ordered her to sit and wait while she 'checked' things out. After having to wait at least forty-five minutes, sitting on a cold, dirty bench, the guard with the glitter lashes called her up to the counter. "You know there's no need to have an attitude."

That's when Stacy started to count to ten. She didn't move, afraid that if she did, she'd do something dangerous.

"Your class is located in the cafeteria," Glitter Lashes continued. "It's way in the back."

There were no apologies, her tone bored and dismissive. Stacy began to count to twenty, but still didn't move.

"Are you deaf or something? I told you where you need to go."

Stacy knew where she wanted to tell this woman to go. But obviously she was already in hell so it didn't matter. This was the guard's domain. She was under her control and had to respect her influence. At one time in her life she'd dined with multi-millionaires and celebrities. How could her life have come to this?

"Is something wrong with you?" Glitter Lashes snapped.

"No," Stacy said in cool voice. She glanced again at the corkscrew curls on the woman's head half expecting them to move like snakes. *I'm sorry Medusa. I just took one look at you and turned to stone.* "Thank you for your help," she said trying her hardest not to sound sarcastic.

"You're welcome," Glitter Lashes said then, to Stacy's amazement, she smiled as if genuinely pleased by Stacy's words and she suddenly looked more human. "And I mean it. Watch your attitude in there or they'll eat you alive."

"I'll remember that," Stacy said softening her tone and this time when she added a quick 'thanks' she meant it.

Stacy passed by the first guard to an area where all her belongings were searched--even a body search, which she found humiliating. Although the male guard used a metal wand, and didn't physically touch her, she felt his eyes, and those of his colleagues undress her. She cringed at the thought of having to go through this process every time she came to teach the class for the next twelve weeks. She almost wished the woman with the corkscrew curls had come with her. By the time she found the sign to the cafeteria, her mood had plummeted.

The women clearly didn't want to be there and neither did she. Her course wasn't mandatory. Most of the women who'd signed up just wanted to get out of their cell. The Vernon County Women's Detention Center was a minimum security facility, that in some ways, looked like a college campus, but the bars, security gates, and uniformed guards never let one forget where you were. Based on her research, the majority of the women were there due to drugs, prostitution, petty crimes or parole violations. But she didn't care. She just wanted her ninety day sentence to be over. There were a total of twenty women in her class and one guard, a man who's eyes she didn't like.

To her surprise, half of her students seemed to have African heritage. The rest were a mixture of Latin American, North American Anglo and one she didn't even dare to guess. One of the woman looked barely out of high school with unnatural red hair and dark roots, making her wonder how someone's daughter ended up here. Stacy knew they hadn't heard of her, but that wasn't a surprise. She made a lot of money, but wasn't a household name. She liked it that way. She didn't want to be known. She liked being able to go where she wanted, without being recognized.

"I'll watch your stuff for you," an older woman said meeting her at the door. The woman looked haggard--like life had punched her in the face and stepped on her just to make a point. She had a flat face, with hanging jowls, puffy eyes and gray, wiry hair. But under the sagging skin Stacy could detect a lovely bone structure and imagined that she'd once been quite a looker in her youth.

"My stuff?" Stacy asked.

"Yes, you can't be too trusting around here. My name's Priscilla."

"Thanks."

Stacy soon found out that, in addition to not trusting them, she couldn't even be heard. For the first fifteen minutes the women continued several conversations and totally ignored her. The correctional officer was of no use, and made no attempt to assist her in gaining control. After trying to get their attention by introducing herself,

Stacy finally sat down and just looked at them. The women soon became quiet.

"Are you going to just sit there?" one called out to her as if she were sitting across a stadium instead of only a few yards away. Her words were coarse, traced with a Brooklyn accent, but she had the command of a queen and the looks to match. She had the East African beauty of a tribal princess. Her black hair was shaved short, her eyes rimmed with dark lashes and her slender frame lounged like a lazy cat.

Stacy rested her chin in her hand and fought back a yawn. "Isn't that what you want?"

"Hell, this is supposed to be some kind of writing class," another women shouted.

"And I thought I was going to get students who understood English, but I was wrong," she mumbled.

The cat sat up straighter and narrowed her eyes. "What do you mean?"

"What?"

"You think we don't speak English. Are you making fun of us?"

Stacy looked around the room. Damn, she hadn't expected to be overheard. "I was just talking to myself, but now that I've got your attention let's talk about the power of a story."

"No, first we want to hear what you meant."

Stacy just stared at her, knowing that silence was her best weapon. This cat wasn't going to let this mouse go, she smelled a kill.

"Come on," Priscilla said. "Let her talk or she'll send us back to our cells."

The cat sent Stacy an ugly look then sat back.

Stacy breathed a sigh of relief then started the first lesson.

~

AT HOME, Stacy went straight to the kitchen, remembering the email from her housekeeper Kelly Bremmer, giving her instructions for dinner. She went to the fridge and popped the premade meal into the microwave. As she waited for it to warm, she looked around her enormous kitchen, which was about the size of her first apartment. She never thought she'd live so well when she'd gone to New York to get her career off the ground. She'd had an average middle class upbringing in a quaint Maryland suburb before she'd met Marshall Harrington, an aspiring actor. She'd gone to New York to write plays. She was only twenty-two, he was twenty-six and a budding stage star. They'd met at an Improv class. She'd been dazzled by how different he was from everyone else. He wasn't loquacious and had the wounded hunger of a true artist. At times moody, but mostly passionate. Passionate about life and art. He made her see life in a whole new way. He shared his hopes and dreams and she felt privileged that he'd chosen her as a confidante. She quickly became protective of him--this talented man who'd kicked a drug and alcohol addiction at twenty-one determined to be the greatest actor of his generation.

She didn't want his genius to be ignored. She even wrote a play for him. Little knowing that soon writing would be the only thing that would save them both. She'd married him too soon, now that she thought about it. Just five months after a whirlwind affair. It wasn't long before she realized that his wounded hunger was more an act than a reality. She learned a year after they'd married, that the life he'd told her about had been a lie. He'd never done drugs or alcohol and his parents had disowned him. Yet, in spite of this, she still convinced herself that she was the only one who could help him, the one person who truly understood him. She accepted and believed that his lies were a cover for a gifted man with a fragile spirit.

But as that fragile spirit grew more demanding of her time, attention and energy-- sucking her joy like an emotional vampire--Stacy turned to her writing as a means of escape. During the first several months of their marriage, he had looked for work and managed to find small parts, but then drew into himself, because the roles weren't big enough and didn't showcase his talent. She got him auditions, but then learned that talent wasn't enough.

He didn't want to put in the effort. He'd been a child of privilege and expected everything to come easily to him. He hated criticism, so he started to sabotage her efforts. She'd left the theater and gotten a 'real job' to support them both, since he wouldn't lower himself to do anything but commit full time to his art. He'd die for his art and at times chastised her for not feeling the same. "It's because you don't' know what it's like to be a true artist. A writer can hide behind her words, a musician behind his music, but an actor must give it his all. My body is my instrument."

She pushed her dreams of writing aside and worked various jobs--waitress, administrative assistant, cashier--because she'd convinced herself that he was more talented. Then she wrote a play that got produced by a local stage company. He dismissed her acclaim by mentioning it was 'easier for a woman'. Especially a pretty one. To combat his painful remark she produced an indie film for him to play the lead in. It received global recognition when she entered it in an international competition--the script and direction getting a lot of notice--to Marshall's annoyance--but when the role didn't lead to the exposure Marshall expected, he deemed the success a failure.

She offered to write another script for him, but he refused saying that her cheap commercial tricks were undermining his true artistic aspirations. He soon began wearing a halo of bitter dreams--hopes deferred. Every conversation becoming as painful as stale dialogue in a static 50's movie with only one subject: his wasted genius.

He was good at making her feel guilty for her success. Reminding her, often, that she was just luckier than he was. Not talented, just luckier. Not harder working, just lucky. Three years into the marriage, when he refused to do anymore small films or theater work or even go on auditions, Stacy decided to pour her misery into a novel. A novel, the first in a mystery series, about a cold case and a detective with ties to a ruthless South African gang. She sent the manuscript off and was surprised when she'd given up hope that it would ever sell, a small publisher made her an offer. The novel didn't take off right away. Sales were barely visible at first, but the publisher was

willing to build her career, which she later found out was
rare in the world of publishing, which spits out writers
like a hungry monster spitting out the bones of its prey. It
wasn't until the fourth book in the series when her financial future turned around. Soon she was licensing foreign
and movie rights and signed a contract for a TV show
based on the characters. But, the brighter her light
became, the darker his moods.

They briefly moved to Washington, DC and found
the artistic community welcoming. But after only six
months Marshall felt it was a waste so they returned to
New York. She tried to make him feel better by dedi-
cating books to him, mentioning his support. But he
continued to make dismissive remarks about her accom-
plishments the more success and praise came her way.
Little did she know that he'd use those efforts against her.
He'd said he'd make her pay if she ever divorced him and
he'd been true to his word. In court he said he had done
extensive research for the books, and managed all the
money. Everyone she thought she could call a friend had
testified against her and supported his claims. He'd been
charming and she'd been left friendless.

During the divorce, they'd painted her as a diva belit-
tling her husband because he hadn't been as successful as
she had. She'd learned how many of their friends had
been jealous and delighted in seeing her fall. They'd all
gone on the side of the winner and Marshall had definitely won. He'd never have to work another day in his
life. And he could get credit for her success. She also
knew that a supportive man was very en vogue and
women would clamor after him. He appeared so loving

and caring, when all he really was, was a parasite. And she'd loved him, that's what burned her the most. She'd loved him and wondered if he'd ever loved her.

Stacy tried to eat, but then started to taste her tears and pushed the plate away. There was no use feeling sorry for herself, although she felt like a failure in everything; her career, her love life. She used to feel so sure of herself and now she didn't know who she was anymore. She'd made a mistake and chosen the wrong man and the wrong life and wished she could be given a second chance with someone else--a chance to be someone else. She looked around at her opulent surroundings. The grand estate had been for him; the cars, the clothes just so he could show off to people. She never needed it. Now he had the money and all the toys he wanted and she paid the bills. She wasn't broke, she'd invested well, but she couldn't write. That had been something that had made her feel whole and alive. Her creative side felt dead and had been so for three years.

She lived like a recluse. But she wouldn't anymore. She would sell the grand house, she didn't even know why she'd kept it this long.

Instead of finishing her dinner, Stacy decided to go up to the attic and look through some of her things. Maybe she could find something that could help her inspire and motivate the women in her class. She was tired of feeling down. She wanted a change, but didn't know how to make it happen. Everything seemed set. She was in a rut, her life turning into a living grave. She searched through a stack of papers packed in a small wooden box, when a small, green leather diary fell out.

Stacy looked at it with amazement. She hadn't seen it in years. She couldn't believe she'd kept it. She hurried back downstairs and sat on her bed and opened in.

"*He loves me so much. Today he took me ballroom dancing...and later, in the evening, we had a romantic dinner on a river cruise and...*"

"*One of my scripts was made into an award winning production and he treated me to a five-star dinner at the Waldorf Astoria in New York City.*"

"*T.P. asked me to marry him.*"

Stacy wiped her tears away and laughed. T.P? She wondered who she'd been thinking about then. What she had written seemed so far away. Had she made up someone or had it been someone she'd really imagined being with? She remembered creating this fake diary when she'd felt that her real life was no longer something to write about. She'd started writing in it after moving to DC, embellishing the entries the more unhappy she became. In this diary she had a man who loved and cherished her and supported all her efforts. They traveled together and laughed and loved. Oh, how she wished she could have lived this life instead. She closed her eyes and hugged the diary to her chest. She wanted a second chance. She wanted to fall in love again and learn how to laugh again. She wanted to reclaim the woman she'd once been. She wanted to prove that she could be a success, without Marshall, and prove to everyone that what he'd said about her had been a lie. Stacy opened her eyes and sighed then tossed the diary in a side drawer and closed it. She had to be realistic. Nothing would change

CHAPTER THREE

HELL NOT ONLY HAD A SMELL, it had a queen. And her name was Laurice Hanover. She disrupted the class even more than last time, leaving Stacy feeling the weight of her sentence. She left the cafeteria eager to put the day behind her and made a wrong turn. She was about to correct herself when she heard barking puppies. She looked across the courtyard and saw a group of inmates walking with several dogs.

"Grab him!" a woman shouted.

Stacy saw a brown ball rush past her and then into the parking lot, narrowly missing getting hit by a car backing out. The busy parking lot was a dangerous place and Stacy knew the brown Labrador mix was going to get hit if someone didn't grab it. Stacy raced after it then stopped. If she chased it, it may think it was a game. She stopped and whistled loud. The puppy stopped. "Stay", she said. To her surprise, the puppy didn't move. She approached it. The puppy's tail began to wag, but she ignored it. She didn't want to reward bad behavior by petting it, although it was adorable. She bent down and took its leash then said, "Come," and the puppy followed.

The woman looked at her grateful. "I can't believe I let Houdini get away again."

"Houdini?"

"Yes," the woman said with a laugh. She had silver hair and a thin Nordic look with beautifully manicured fingers. "He wants to get out of this place just like most of the women, but I'm not sure he's suited for this course. I found him and wanted to give him a chance, but he's too much to handle."

"He's smart and knows commands," Stacy said impressed by how calm the puppy stayed beside her.

"Maybe you have a better knack with him than we do. He actually looks good on you."

Stacy shook her head. "Oh no, I couldn't have a dog."

"Why not? You're a natural."

"I'd like to hear more about your program," Stacy said eager to change the subject.

"Sure, by the way, my name's Nila. This program helps to give the women skills they can use on the outside. Some work in shelters, animal hospitals, vet clinics and other places. Having skills like relating to others and patience, can be useful in any line of work. It gives them something to do and something to love. Both animal and human heal."

"Sounds wonderful. "

"I think so. It was a fight to get the program started but we've been going strong five years now."

Nila led Stacy, and Houdini into a small office. They

sat and shared some coffee. "Would your husband object to you having a dog?"

"Oh, I'm not married. Thank God that's over," Stacy added with a bitter laugh. "It's not that. I just don't have room in my life for a dog."

"Boyfriend?"

"What?"

"Do you have a boyfriend?"

Stacy frowned. "No, but I don't see--"

"He needs you and you need him. I can always tell a perfect match when I see one."

"I'm sorry but--"

"Just give him a week, if he doesn't grow on you by then give him back to me."

It seemed reasonable and Stacy did like him. And she thought it would be nice to fill the house with a companion. Something she could trust. "Okay." She bent down and stroked the puppy who slept soundly, exhausted from his recent escapade.

"So how come?"

Stacy frowned. "How come what?"

"You're not seeing anyone. I know it's a personal question, but I'm just curious."

"Are you married?"

"Yes."

"Happily?"

Nila grinned. "Oh is that it? You married a piece of trash and hate mankind?"

"I don't hate men. I don't have the energy. I just haven't met the right one yet."

"Do you want to?"

Stacy lifted her brows in feigned surprise. "Are you offering?"

"If I swung the other way I'd be hitting on you. You're attractive, you're smart, you're kind." She finished her coffee and set the empty cup on the table.

Stacy sniffed. No one had called her attractive in years. "Not many men think so. My ex didn't and I did a horrible thing to some guy's car. I've been thinking I'll take myself off the market for a while."

"Thinking and doing are two different things." Nila pulled out a little black book and started scribbling down some notes. "You're interested in someone now, aren't you?"

Stacy watched her with interest. "What are you doing?"

"Just got a great idea I want to write down before I lose it." She looked up at Stacy and winked. "As a writer, I'm sure you know how that feels."

"How did you know I'm a writer?"

"Prisons have ears. I heard about the new program that you're part of. I think it's great."

"It wasn't my idea."

"It's still great. So what kind of man do you want?"

"We're back to that?"

"Just pretend. Come on, you're a writer, use your imagination."

Stacy hesitated, lifting her coffee cup then setting it back down. She sighed. "He doesn't exist."

Nila's grin grew. "Say it anyway."

"A man who's successful in his own right and won't

be jealous of my success, but proud. And confident. Considerate and can laugh at himself."

"Ambitious but carefree?"

Stacy frowned. "I told you he doesn't exist."

Nila shrugged. "You'd be surprised." She put her black book away. "I hope things work out with you and Houdini."

"Thanks." Stacy looked down at Houdini and hoped so too.

～

ROCKETT LOOKED around the elegant hotel room enjoying the scent of the fresh sheets and expensive cologne before she let her gaze settle on the man who sat on the bed. She'd been warned about him. He liked it rough and hard. Fortunately she was a professional and was prepared. He was better looking than she'd expected. The men who hired her usually didn't look this good or weren't this young. She knew he was a doctor, but that was all she needed or wanted to know. He probably had a wife, or a girlfriend, who didn't know his real desire, that was fine with her. Those women kept her in business. He wasn't a talker, which was a relief. The talkers bored her, although they were usually easier to please. The show *Heartbeat* was on the TV, and she reached to turn it off, even though it was one of her favorite shows.

"Leave it," he said.

She grinned at him. "And if I don't?"

He snatched the remote from her and set it aside.

She shrugged. Each man was different and she'd take

his lead on the game he wanted to play. She knew he liked to dole out punishment and that was what she was there for. She soon discovered he didn't like toys, so he ignored the chains, the handcuffs and the whip, preferring to use his hands to slap and scratch her. He was harder, faster, rougher and more vicious than she'd expected, but she was a professional and didn't let her surprise show.

When he wrapped his hands around her neck and squeezed, she welcomed the sexual high of suffocation, but before she slipped into dark unconsciousness she saw the rage in his eyes. Quickly her arousal was enveloped by fear and for a brief moment, she wondered if she'd ever see daylight again.

∼

Stacy sat alone in a restaurant, eating her way through a chocolate mousse wanting to forget her miserable day at the detention center. She'd dropped Houdini at home later that day, to be looked after by Kelly, before treating herself. As she stared at her chocolate mousse the man she'd met with laughing, dark brown eyes came into her mind. She wished she knew the words to describe them. Although he had a rough exterior, with his beard and shabby clothes, he was sexy. If it had been another time she would have flirted with him, although she was terribly out of practice and doubted he'd be interested. Maybe it was good she'd met him only briefly. She might have made an idiot of herself otherwise. He was the kind of man who could walk into a room, choose a corner, and with just one look, catch the eye of a woman and make her come to him.

He had that cool, sophisticated energy of a seducer who with a look could cast a spell. A man like that would be dangerous to her. Besides, she didn't want to go from one man who'd blinded her to another who made her heart race, no matter how attracted she was to him. Keeping a man like that interested would take a lot of work anyway. He likely had plenty of women eager to keep his attention. Marshall had shown her how a wedding band didn't matter. But even though she'd never be with a man like the stranger, Stacy couldn't help imagining being with someone like him. What would it be like? What would it be like to have his steady gaze locked with hers. To be his?

The vibration of her cell phone interrupted her thoughts. She answered. "Hello?"

"Sis, you've got to help me," her younger brother Franklin said.

The tone of his voice sent shivers through her. She gripped the phone and her heart raced, but she kept her voice calm. "Why?"

"It's all gone."

"What's all gone?"

"The money. The investments. It's gone," he said, then told her about a project he'd invested their parent's money in. "What am I going to do? They'll lose everything."

"I told you to be careful and conservative when it came to investing their money."

"I know, I just thought I had a sure thing."

"What do you expect me to do?"

"Help me. Help us. I know you have money."

"Not as much as I used to, especially after the divorce."

"Stacy please."

"I'll call you back tomorrow."

"You can't let them know about this."

"Don't worry, I'll think of something." She hung up. How could this have happened? He was supposed to look after their parents and now they could lose all the things they'd struggled to build since coming to this country from Jamaica.

Stacy quickly rushed into the bathroom and lost her meal. It didn't take long since she hadn't eaten much. Unfortunately, she still couldn't write. What could she do? She'd have to sell things. She'd already planned to sell the grand house and the cars, she'd keep her condo, but the money wouldn't last long. Her life was swirling down the drain. She left the bathroom stall and met the startled brown gaze she'd been dreaming about.

CHAPTER FOUR

"What are you doing in the ladies' room?" Stacy demanded.

Chance folded his arms and smiled amused. "Actually, it's the men's room."

Stacy turned and saw the urinals and two men who were putting them to good use.

Her face burned. She wished she could crumble into a ball and disappear. "I'm so sorry," she said in a rush then raced out. She quickly settled her bill then stumbled out of the restaurant onto the busy sidewalk, surprised her legs could still hold her up. The day was going from bad to worse. All she needed now was lightning to strike her down. She thought of the stock market crash and men jumping from buildings. She knew how they felt.

She walked aimlessly against the wave of people pushing past her. She stepped into the road. A strong hand violently yanked her back and she felt the breeze from a car speeding past her. It chilled the sweat on her skin.

"Do you have a death wish or something?"

Stacy spun around and looked up into the familiar brown eyes again. "Oh no, not you. Please, leave me alone." She tried to push him away, but his grip tightened.

"Come on, you need to sit down." He didn't give her a chance to argue. He led her to an outside table.

"You look pale," he said, handing her a glass of water. She didn't even remember it arriving. "Do you need a doctor?"

"No," Stacy said, feeling as if she were in a fog and all her movements were in slow motion. *I need a miracle.* She stood.

"Sit down."

"I'm all right."

He tugged her back down. "Is there a friend I can call?"

"Why are you being nice to me?"

"Do you want me to get you a cab?"

She shook her head. "Please stop being nice to me. Call me names, tell me I'm pathetic or crazy."

"Why?"

"Then you'll be in sync with how my day has been."

"Maybe it's time for things to change," he said. His amused brown gaze seemed to plead for friendship, which Stacy couldn't understand. Then he did something that was her complete undoing. His mouth curved into a soft smile. She could have taken anything but that genuine, warm smile. A smile that said everything would be okay, that you're not crazy. She couldn't understand why he made her feel that, no matter how bad life got, she would be fine, that she could trust him. Why did he seem so familiar? He still looked rugged and sexy and she didn't usually go for men with beards. Why couldn't she have met a man like him before her life was ruined? Before she met Marshall? Before she'd trusted her brother to look after their parents? Despair tore at her heart and tears slowly made their way down her face.

His smile disappeared and his gaze sharpened. "Tell me what's wrong."

"I can't," she said in a choked voice craving his kindness but also wishing he wasn't so kind.

"Why not?"

"I don't even know you."

"Yes, you do," he said with a vehemence that surprised her.

She shook her head ashamed. "I know I should, but I don't. Tell me your name maybe I'll know you then."

"Chance Jamison," he said slowly, his gaze clinging to her as if studying her reaction.

Stacy bit her lip and glanced up at the sky. His name rang a bell, but she still couldn't place him. She shrugged. "It's a nice name."

A brief look of disappointment crossed his face then disappeared. "Forget it, Stacy." He leaned back in his chair. "So, now can you tell me what's wrong?"

She wiped her eyes with the back of her hand. "No."

"Okay, then can you help me?"

She looked at him in surprise. "Help you?"

He nodded.

"Do what?"

"I want to go to Madame Tussauds but I don't want to go by myself. All my friends are busy and it'd be nice to act like a tourist. I think it will help take your mind off your troubles and you'd be doing me a favor."

"I'm sorry, but I can't," Stacy said then her phone rang and she saw it was her mother. "Excuse me," she said then answered. "Hello?" she said expecting to hear her mother in tears.

"If your brother calls you, don't give him any money."

"What?"

"He's in a lot of trouble, but this time he's got to get out of it himself."

Stacy paused. "Wait...what?"

"I've tried to keep this from you since you were going through your divorce, but your brother has been stealing from us. After we stopped allowing him access to our estate he buried himself in debt elsewhere and he's scrambling to find a way out."

"So he hasn't been investing your money?"

Her mother laughed. "Not for a long time now."

Stacy gripped the phone. *That slimy little eel.* "So your investments are fine?"

"Perfectly fine. Just be warned, he'll want money from me. I love my son but I'm afraid we spoiled him a little too much."

"Thanks," Stacy said not wanting her mother to feel worse than she did. "I'll remember. Bye." She disconnected. So her brother was in trouble and wanted to be rescued--again. This time he'd be in for a surprise. She looked up at Chance and reconsidered his offer. Her first instinct was to say no. She hadn't gone out with a man in over three years, but her brother's lie made her angry and she didn't want to be angry anymore. She wanted to have fun. Her brother had ruined her meal but she wouldn't let him ruin her day. "Okay," she said feeling suddenly reckless. "Let's go."

And she had more fun than she'd ever imagined. Stacy explored the museum with Chance, experiencing it in a way she never had the last time she'd visited. He made her laugh and relax, amazing her with his extensive knowledge on various topics. Soon her troubles became a memory. Afterwards he took her to a corner restaurant where the wait staff greeted him as if he were family. They sat at a table where he treated her to a New York-style pizza and talked about the Madame Tussauds in England, where they'd both travelled. It surprised her that they had a lot in common: They had similar tastes in music, past times and love of the arts. She told him about her writing background and, to test him, told him about her bestselling series. To her pleasure he was impressed. "You didn't say it," she said with a laugh.

"Say what?"

"That you want to write, or that you have written. Every time I mention that I write someone tells me that they want to write too."

He shook his head. "No, never had the desire, but I respect the craft."

A middle aged woman, wearing a peach colored baseball cap approached the table and tapped Chance on the shoulder. When he looked up at her she bent down and whispered, "Be careful of your brother."

His face spread into a wide smile that made the woman blush. "Thanks, I will."

The woman patted his shoulder then left.

"You have a real community here," Stacy said impressed, although she found the warning odd. "People know you and worry about you."

He shrugged. "I like it. It can get awkward at times, but when I'm here, I don't have the same hassles as others."

She nodded, not quite knowing what he meant.

Chance leaned forward, resting his arms on the table, his gaze growing intent. "So are you ready now?"

Stacy swallowed feeling her skin grow warm. "Ready?"

"Yes, to tell me what happened."

"No."

"Maybe another time?"

He wanted to see her again? This attractive, funny, smart man wanted to see her again? She felt like dancing, but feigned nonchalance. "Maybe."

Chance stood and put on the baseball cap he'd bought from a street vendor. "Good. Let me walk you home."

"I have to take the subway," she lied. Her car was parked in an underground parking garage, but she didn't want the day to end and hated the thought of saying goodbye. She'd pay whatever price she had to when she picked it up later.

"That's okay, unless you're trying to get rid of me."

Stacy grinned. No, she certainly didn't want to do that. "Let's go."

~

"I'm so glad you're not one of those," Stacy said in a low voice as the subway train rumbled to a stop at a station and two men got off. She'd overheard them talking. One mentioned his job as a bartender and the other talked about a possible audition.

"One of what?" Chance said with a frown.

"One of those two guys."

"Do you have something against bartenders? I was one once."

"I'd dated a guy who tended bar briefly. He was an aspiring writer. I guess that's no surprise. A lot of people come to New York to hit it big. But that's not what I mean. I mean, I'm glad you're not an actor. I'm off of actors."

He paused. "Why?"

"My ex was one and all his friends too. I've been surrounded by needy, self-interested, shallow people for more than I want to remember. Now I want to be with people who are grounded in the real world. Who actually care about what happens in other parts of the globe and not who's dating whom and who's wearing what or what angle is their best side."

Chance laughed, but it sounded a little strained. "Not all actors are like that."

"No, there are different ones of course. The elitist snobs of the stage and the vapid sirens of the screen."

His brows shot up. "Wow, that's rather harsh."

"I'm in a harsh mood. Oh, this is my stop."

Once they were aboveground again Chance said, "I've

met some awful actors myself but, they're not all like that. As a whole actors--"

"Are a group unto themselves," Stacy finished. "Guys like you wouldn't understand that."

He tapped his chest. "Guys like me?"

"Yes. Every second sentence isn't about you--it's refreshing."

"Thanks, but as a matter of fact--"

"You're so good natured and down to earth. I told you that I'm a writer and you didn't start asking about who I've worked with or if there's something you could see. You don't care about the directors I know. You don't have that calculating ambition in your eyes. I've told myself I'll never date another actor again."

Chance fell so silent the next several blocks that Stacy regretted her words. Maybe he thought she was too judgmental or condescending. What if he had a friend who was an actor? She didn't want him to think that she'd treat him poorly. "It's not something I usually talk about," she said quickly. "It's just that I feel I can trust you. I know your friend is a producer so you probably have lots of friends who are actors."

Chance shoved his hands in his pockets. "Hmm"

"So what do you do?" she asked, eager to get him talking again.

Chance stared ahead. "How far is your place?"

Stacy pointed to a building up ahead. It was a condo she used when she was in town. Her good mood plummeted. He wanted to get rid of her. He probably wouldn't call her and she didn't blame her. She should have kept her thoughts to herself until she'd gotten to know him better. But maybe it was for the best. She needed to find someone who was not in the industry. "We're here." She held out her hand. "Thanks for a great day."

Chance glanced down at her hand then playfully swatted it away. "I'm walking you to your door."

"You don't have to do that."

He sighed. "Are you really going to pretend that you want me to leave?"

A grin tugged on the side of her mouth. "No, but don't expect anything. You're just walking me to my door. I'm not inviting you in."

He looked up at the building. "What floor do you live on?"

"The tenth."

He grinned and winked at her, making her heart leap. "Then I have nine floors to change your mind."

And he playfully did so all the way up the elevator and as they walked down the hall. Stacy giggled at his exaggerated attempts to get her to let him in as she turned her key in the door. "And the answer is still no."

Chance nodded. "I tried."

"It was a good effort," she said then opened the door and stifled a scream.

CHAPTER FIVE

"Houdini got loose," Kelly said holding the puppy by the leash. "I just caught him. The bathroom's the worst--I don't think you should go in there," Kelly said as Stacy marched past.

"I want to see it," Stacy said, then regretted the decision when she saw the destruction.

Kelly stopped behind her and shook her head, dismayed. "I'd hoped to have it cleaned up before you got home. I'd confined him to the kitchen so that I could run some errands, but he must have gotten loose."

Stacy looked around and saw what Houdini had done. This was the second time he'd gotten loose, and destroyed things. This time, he had taken hold of several of her prized lipsticks and the damage was evident on her camel leather couch, the Persian wool rug she'd been given as a gift from a gracious actor, and smeared into the Italian marble tiles in the bathroom.

"You need to see your bedroom," Kelly said.

Stacy hesitated, then stormed into her bedroom, pulling a reluctant Houdini by the leash behind her. He was refusing to walk, and she could tell by his posture that he knew he was in big trouble. Her clothes were strewn all over, several of her dresses were ripped, and he had chewed through three pairs of shoes. Stacy gripped her hands and screamed. Houdini yanked so hard on his leash, his collar broke. He dashed under the bed. Stacy threw the leash on the ground and stomped on it. "I should have known my day would end like this! I should never have gotten a dog. What was I thinking? Why did I let her con me into this?" She shook her fists at the ceiling. "Enough already! I have a lying brother, a she devil for a student, a bastard for an ex and I now own a Tasmanian devil for a dog. All I need is for lightning to strike me."

Chance grabbed her wrist. "You don't want that."

She stared up at him, stunned he was still there. She'd forgotten about him. She yanked her hand free. "You don't know me that well."

His gaze hardened. "Calm down."

"Don't tell me what to do in my own house," she snapped, embarrassment making her tone harsh. "He has to go! I brought him here out of the goodness of my heart and this is how I'm repaid," she said patting her chest. "This is what happens when you try to do something nice. When you care about something else besides yourself. I let him into my house, my space and he just takes advantage of me. Destroying things that are important to me. He doesn't care. He doesn't think about anyone else but himself. He's selfish and he has to go."

Chance lifted a brow, resting his hands on his hips. "We're not talking about the dog anymore, are we?"

"Of course we are," Stacy said stumbling over the words.

He shook his head. "Look at him."

"I can hardly see him under the bed."

"Yes, you can," Chance said his voice firm. "Try again."

Stacy looked under the bed and this time she did see Houdini-- shivering, evidence of his terror --- a puddle of pee. Damn, she hadn't meant to terrify him. Nila was wrong, they weren't good for each other. She'd tried three trainers, bought books and digital courses on housetraining a puppy and still he was destructive. Not only did he destroy things, but what she hated most was him racing out the door every time she came home, and having to chase him down the hallway.

"Is that the reaction you want?" Chance said, pointing at the puppy.

Stacy straightened feeling guilty and embarrassed that he'd witnessed her outburst. "No, but--"

"He's bored. He's not being selfish. He's young and has energy to burn and he's frustrated. He's not doing this to you on purpose."

"Do you want a dog? You can have him. He wouldn't know the difference anyway. Feed and shelter him and he'll be loyal to you. Take him. He deserves a new home."

"No."

"Then I'm taking him to a shelter."

"No, you won't."

"Yes, I will." Stacy folded her arms. "Stop telling me what to do."

Chance looked at her for a moment, concerned. "Why are you so angry?"

"You know why I'm angry. He ruined everything!"

Chance shook his head, keeping his voice soft. "No, he didn't. Tell me what's really making you angry."

She gestured to the room. "Look at this mess."

But he didn't look at the mess instead he continued to stare at her.

"Go home."

His jaw twitched, but he didn't move.

Stacy covered her face, unable to meet his assessing gaze. She thought of the custom made bed she'd bought for Houdini, the assortment of toys and treats. She'd even cleared a special spot for him in her office. She'd hired a dog walker to take Houdini for long walks, but nothing mattered. She couldn't even make a ten month old puppy happy. But she didn't want to admit that failure to Chance. "I don't want to be used again. I won't ever let that happen. I won't let someone make me a doormat or a dishrag again. I won't." She took a deep breath feeling more in control. She let her hands fall and glared at him. "This is my house and I make the rules. The dog is going and you can't stop me."

Chance knelt down and coaxed Houdini to come to him then held the puppy up and waved one of his paws. He made his voice sound like a little child's. "Mommy, I'm sorry. I didn't mean to make you angry."

"Stop that," Stacy said annoyed by how adorable both man and puppy looked.

"Please, don't send me away."

"Chance," Stacy said, irritated that she could already feel her heart softening.

"I promise I'll be better. You're the best Mommy I've ever had."

She folded her arms and shook her head, trying hard not to smile. "No."

Chance made his voice higher and his eyes wide like a hurt little boy. "Pleaseeee?"

"I said stop it."

"Uncle Chance will help us get along. Pretty pleaseee...."

Stacy rolled her eyes then laughed feeling her anger subside. "You're incorrigible."

Chance dropped his voice to his regular level. "Does that mean Houdini gets to stay?"

"Why do you care so much?"

"I asked first."

"I'll give him a reprieve." She held up a finger to make a point. "Just this once, but if he does something like this again he...why are you shaking your head?"

"Because he's young and he's going to make a mistake. If you're not going to keep him then it's best you stop now. Does he have a home here or not?"

"You're not being fair."

Chance blinked at her stunned. "I'm not being fair? Did you hear yourself a minute ago? Your puppy got into your makeup case and you went off on him like he was an ex-husband. Didn't you see him trembling?"

"Well, I--"

"Or maybe that was just me. For a moment I pictured you with a sledgehammer--"

Stacy covered his mouth with one hand and pointed at him with the other. "Don't bring that up again," she warned in a low voice.

Chance removed her hand, unfazed by her biting tone. "Has anyone ever told you that you may have some anger issues?"

Stacy sighed knowing he was right. "Okay, maybe I went a little overboard."

Chance's brows shot up. "A little?" He folded his arms. "Do I need to remind you what you did to my car?"

Stacy shook her fists at him. "Why do you keep bringing that up? Besides it wasn't your car and--"

"I'm worried about you."

Stacy stared at him openmouthed. "Worried?"

"Yes, you get angry at the wrong things and in scary ways. Did you ever fight like this with your ex-husband?"

"No." He usually shouted at her, and she stayed silent. She always stayed silent. She only fought back on the page. Deep inside a story was where she felt most herself. "And I have a right to be angry, but you don't understand because you never get angry."

"Of course I do."

"When? I've never seen it."

Chance flashed a quick grin. "You don't know me that well either."

"But you've had plenty of opportunity to lose your temper and you didn't."

He shrugged. "I'm not saying you shouldn't get angry.

But you shouldn't be like a Lamborghini going from zero to a hundred in three seconds."

"See?" She leaned against the wall. "I told you I'm not good for him. I'm terrible. I have the emotional stability of a volcano."

Chance frowned. "I didn't say that."

"But that's what you mean. I'm irrational. I have hidden baggage that I'm not dealing with. A therapist told me that once. That's why I have few friends. That's why I'm teaching creative writing to women in detention. That's why a judge ordered me to pay my lousy ex alimony because I'm just not likeable and...where are you going?" She asked when he turned and started to walk away. She followed him. "Oh, did I make you angry? I'm sorry I should be more demur." She watched him grab a glass and go to the sink. He filled it with water and ignored her. "An angry woman is scary to a man," she said.

He turned and threw the water in her face.

She stared at him stunned.

He looked down at the glass with regret. "Damn, I thought you'd melt."

Stacy wiped water from her eyes. "I can't believe you just did that."

"Feel better now?"

"No."

He turned to the sink.

She grabbed his arm. "Don't even think about it."

"I'm thirsty."

She tried to wrestle the glass from him. "No, you're not."

He moved the glass out of reach. "Yes, I am."

"Then drink somewhere else."

"You want me to leave?"

"Yes."

"And if I don't?"

"I'll make you."

A slow grin spread across his face. "I'd like to see you try."

Stacy grabbed a butcher knife. "Will this persuade you?"

Chance opened his arms wide. "Take your aim." He pointed to his jugular vein. "Slice this and I won't last long."

Stacy let her arms fall to her sides and stared at him perplexed. "What is wrong with you?"

He started to laugh.

"What's so funny?"

"You just reminded me of a friend of mine. He's always telling me what's wrong with me. Maybe you should ask him."

She shook her head amazed. "I can't believe you're laughing."

He continued to laugh. "You don't find this funny? You're asking 'What's wrong with me?' And you're holding a butcher knife." He suddenly sobered as if coming to a realization. "Oh...wait a minute. Am I supposed to be scared?"

"Yes. Most men would be."

He nodded as if considering her words. "Is that what you want? You want me to be scared of you?" He reached over and took the knife from her. "Because you don't scare me, Stacy. Not one little bit. Do you know why? Because I know you're not irrational. That you are very likable and that I'm lucky to have you in my life. So you won't be able to drive me away."

"You hardly know me."

His gaze dipped to her lips then returned to her eyes. "I know you better than you think."

"I'm really not a dog person," Stacy swallowed, wondering how he could make her feel so many emotions--anger, annoyance, and attraction.

"Become one."

"Maybe it won't work."

Chance rested his hands on her shoulders. "He needs you and you need him. And you both need me."

"I'll probably regret this."

Chance called Houdini who came running. He sat and Chance gave him a treat. He handed a treat to Stacy. "Now you give him one."

"He doesn't like me."

"He's totally forgotten about the screaming. He's fine now. Just give him a treat."

She did. The puppy gazed up at her and she stroked him and he licked her hand, his tail wagging.

Chance grinned. "He adores you."

"He probably wants another treat."

"Or to be petted more. Not everyone who comes into your life wants something from you."

Stacy kept her gaze lowered not trusting herself to look at him again. "Are you still referring to Houdini?"

"What do you think?"

She straightened. She didn't know what to think.

When she was with him she didn't want to think. That could be dangerous. "I don't know."

Chance drew her close. "I want you to trust me."

"You want me to keep the dog," she said knowing they both were really talking about something else.

"That too. Relax. He likes you."

Stacy searched his eyes--trying to find a hint of deception. Could he really be as attracted to her as she was to him? Was he just another cunning rogue who'd break her heart. "He is adorable," she said with reluctance. *And you're gorgeous.*

"I know a trainer who can help you. And a doggy daycare service."

She bit her lip. Did he really mean he'd stay with her? That he wouldn't judge her? That she could be truly safe with him? Trust him? "Okay."

His gaze dipped to her lips again and for one wild minute she thought he would kiss her, but then he quickly turned. "I'd better go." He headed for the door.

"I thought you said you were thirsty," Stacy said surprised and disappointed by his abrupt change.

"I'll get a drink later," he said in a rush, eager to leave. He opened the door.

"I can't convince you to stay a little longer?" Stacy asked wondering what she'd done wrong.

His bold gaze roved over her in a lazy seductive way and his voice deepened."If I stay a second longer, I'll find a way to spend the night."

Her heart jolted and she gave a nervous laugh, resisting the urge to move closer to him. "That would take a miracle."

He winked. "Hey, I came in, didn't I?" he said, then stole a quick kiss that left her mouth burning. "Bye."

Stacy closed the door then rested against it and touched her lips, wondering what it would have felt like if he had kissed her for more than a second. She felt her whole body grow warm at the thought. She pushed herself from the door and shook her head. She had to take things slow, even though she knew she'd count the days until she could see him again. He'd made a horrible day seem that much better and next time she'd treat him. With that thought in mind, she helped Kelly clean up Houdini's mess, even humming at times.

~

LATER, Stacy walked into her bedroom, exhausted. She overheard Kelly talking to someone. "Yea, Crazy Stacy had a major meltdown today. You should have seen her flip out. Damn, I thought I'd be able to clean up the mess her dog made before she got back. You wouldn't believe the amount of money she's spent on this stupid dog, even wanting me to hire a babysitter. Yea, I know. I just thought if I took the little beast out for it to poop and kept him in the bathroom he'd be fine, but he's like an escape artist. Uh huh...I know. Yea, right. I didn't expect it to be this bad though. This is when I wish she'd kept the house. It would have been easier to hide the dog there than here. But boy you should have seen her face. I wish I'd caught it on camera. She really lost it when she saw what the dog had done."

Kelly was talking about her? Making fun of her? She

was one of the few people she thought she could still trust. Stacy stepped closer to listen more.

"Some guy she brought home had to calm her down. No, I don't know who he was, but probably nobody interesting. She doesn't have many friends or people to talk about. Great body though, but I couldn't really see his face because of the baseball cap. I'm thinking of adding it to my 'Dealing with a Diva' blog. I'll make some changes of course, but the readers are going to eat this up."

Stacy took out her cell phone and accessed the blog. Her heart constricted as she read some of the awful tales Kelly had written about her. Calling her a 'diva' and other less flattering terms.

"The moment we sign that book deal I am out of here. Yea, I better go, I think I hear her. Bye."

Stacy quickly put her phone away then walked into the bathroom to confront her.

Kelly smiled at her as if they were old friends. "Everything is as good as new."

Stacy looked around. Kelly may be a backstabber, but she still was a great housekeeper. She'd trusted her to keep her place in order. "Thank you. I'll bet you can't wait to stop doing this. You want more time to write."

Her smile fell. "What?"

"What did you do with the money for the dog sitter?" She'd given her money to get one, now she knew she'd pocketed the money instead.

"I don't know what you're talking about?"

Stacy sighed. Did everyone close to her lie? "When should I congratulate you about your book deal?"

Kelly blinked fast and stumbled over her words. "Oh, it's really nothing."

"You don't need to wait for the deal to come through, you can leave now."

"Look, you don't understand."

"And I don't care to. Goodbye."

Kelly marched past her. Stacy watched her gather her things then sat in the living room and waited until she heard the front door slam. She took a deep breath and blinked back tears. Kelly's betrayal hurt more than she expected. She could hear Julia telling her that she could sue for libel, if the book or blog warranted it. But she didn't want to spend any more time fighting in court. Lately, everything seemed like a fight. She lay on the couch and let the tears fall. Houdini came up to her and nudged her leg. She gripped her hand into a fist then relaxed and stroked him, feeling her pain ebb a little. "I guess it's just you and me now." She scratched him behind his ear and he closed his eyes in pleasure. "So you were just as angry as me for getting locked up. I'm sorry. It'll be better next time."

Stacy gathered what little energy she had left and looked at her mail. She quickly waded through her bills and junk mail, feeling numb then a beautiful envelope caught her eye.

CHAPTER SIX

INTRIGUED, Stacy turned the envelope over and studied it. It looked like an invitation. She didn't get invitations anymore. Had it come to the wrong address? She checked the label and saw her name: Stacy Regina Price. She grabbed a letter opener and swiftly cut it open. Inside the gold lined envelope was a handwritten note on expensive parchment paper trimmed with finely woven lace. She read: *You have been personally selected to join The Black Stockings Society, an elite, members-only club that will change your life and help you find the man of your dreams. Guaranteed.*

The Black Stockings Society? She'd never heard of it. Was it some kind of lingerie club? How had they gotten her name? She scanned the rest of the note.

Dumped? Bored? Tired of being single? Ready to live dangerously? Then this is the club for you. Guaranteed results! Submit your application today.

Dumped? Yes and no. She'd dumped her husband, but he'd emotionally dumped her years ago.

Tired of being single? Yes and no. She'd just finalized her divorce and hadn't looked at another man. She should be relishing her new singlehood, but after meeting Chance she was rethinking her options. Maybe she was ready for a new relationship. Had Julia given her name to some dating service to cheer her up?

Ready to live dangerously? Stacy paused. She had taken in a dog without thinking and, for one minute, thought of throwing caution to the wind and asking Chance to spend the night. Maybe she was ready to add some adventure to her life.

Guaranteed results, huh? She looked at the nominal fee and application. It wouldn't hurt to try it out. Stacy went over to her desk and pulled out a pen and looked at the enclosed questionnaire. Then frowned with disappointment when she looked at the questions. They didn't make much sense and weren't as analytical and scientific as she would have expected them to be, but she answered them anyway.

How would you spend five dollars? Only five dollars? She didn't remember the last time she'd spent so little. She quickly wrote down 'I don't know' then scratched it out and wrote instead 'Buy something at a pizzeria,' remembering the delicious pizza Chance had bought her.

Do you prefer sugar or salt? Depends on the recipe.

What would your ideal man be like?

Stacy laughed, thinking of Nila. Why did that question keep coming up? She didn't think her ideal man existed, although Chance made her wonder. He came pretty close. But she didn't know him that well. She wrote: 'Sexy, easy to talk to.' She paused then tried to think of something else and wrote down driven. Marshall hadn't been. Once she finished, she read the "sworn oath" at the bottom of the page: *As a member of The Black Stockings Society, I swear I will not reveal club secrets, I will accept nothing but the best and I will no longer settle for less.*

Stacy briefly wondered about the secrecy of the club. She couldn't even tell Julia? She pushed any concerns aside. Her life wasn't the way she wanted and this club signified a welcome change. She'd take whatever help they could give. She wrote a check for the nominal membership fee, signed the application and oath then sealed the envelope and put it in the mail.

To her shock, two days later a medium sized package arrived. The package included four pairs of stockings, a membership card that read Stacy Regina Price, Member, The Black Stockings Society, and also included a set of instructions.

*Welcome to The Black Stockings Society. Your first assignment is to take your membership card to Chic Spa and Hair salon where you will ask for the **deluxe special**. Please set plenty of time aside for this appointment. You'll meet with Damion. Once you have completed this assignment you will wear one of your stockings to your next class at the detention center.*

How did they know she was teaching a class at the detention center? Why would she wear one of the stockings to the class? How would that help her meet her ideal man? But Stacy pushed her concerns aside, she wouldn't pass up an opportunity for a spa treatment. Stacy immediately called and made her appointment then groaned when she saw what else she had on her calendar: Anger Management Class.

~

IT HAD BEEN A CLOSE CALL. Chance set his razor down and stared at his reflection. His beard was gone and days had passed since he'd last seen Stacy, but he still felt like he was running a fever. She'd always had that effect on him, at times making him tongue tied. When he was around her he sometimes felt like a big, awkward kid, but with a laugh she put him at ease and then made him feel like nothing was impossible. It had been so tempting to stay that night, but he'd had to pull himself away. He didn't want to ruin anything. She still didn't recognize him and he wondered when she would--if she would. It was a wound to his pride that she didn't remember anything about him, but then it had only been a brief meeting. Two weeks one summer. She'd forgotten, but meeting her then had changed his life.

He wanted to know who had made her cry. Was it her ex-husband or someone else? Who'd taken her smile from her? Would she give him a chance to bring it back? He was eager to establish a relationship with her, but knew he had to be patient, which was the last thing he wanted to be, now that he'd found her again.

Unfortunately, he had to, especially since she'd changed so much. She hated actors. He silently swore and put on some aftershave. When had that happened?

What would she do when she found out what he was? How could he prove that he was different from other actors? He knew it wouldn't be easy to change her mind. He should have told her, but wanted to wait for the right time. But he wasn't sure when that would be.

~

STACY GLANCED AROUND at the cream colored walls and looked at her Anger Management instructor. Two days of group activities and heartfelt stories made Stacy want to break something. If hell ever froze over, Stacy knew her instructor would reign supreme. Mora Sharpton had the lithe body of a yoga instructor, a sharp Bronx accent, reddish blonde hair, ruddy cheeks and ice blue eyes. So far, Stacy had been able to endure her and was glad she only had one day left. But today when she entered the room she was the only one there. Her instructor Mora glanced over her paper work. "You've got a nasty temper."

I'm not here to get a merit badge, Stacy thought, but kept her mouth shut.

Mora looked up at her. "This is your last day."

Stacy nodded.

A cool smile touched Mora's lips. "Bet you think this is a waste of time."

Stacy sighed.

Mora's smile widened. "You're angry right now, aren't you? You wish you were anywhere else but here."

Stacy folded her arms. She only had to last a few more hours then she'd never have to see this woman again.

"Let's go." Mora took Stacy to another room where a punching bag stood. She tossed her a pair of boxing gloves. "Go ahead and get it out."

"What? You want me to punch it?"

"You're ready for a fight, you might as well finish it and get it out of the way. You either punch that or me. It's your choice."

CHAPTER SEVEN

"I'M NOT GOING to hit you and a punching bag won't make anything any better."

"Have you tried it? Scared?"

"No."

"Then hit it."

Stacy put on the gloves then gave the bag a light punch.

Mora shoved her back hard and she fell down with a thud. "Stop wasting my time."

Stacy stared up at her stunned. "What did you do that for?" She stood.

Mora pushed her again. Harder, causing Stacy to fall down again.

Stacy jumped to her feet. "Stop that."

"Why? I thought you liked being pushed around. You like having a reason to be angry."

"No, I don't."

"You're always ready for a fight so I'm giving you one."

"I never said that," Stacy protested. "I don't want to fight."

"Then why are you always angry?"

"I'm not," Stacy said, trying to keep her temper under control.

"What about your ex?"

"He's a bastard."

"And your lawyer?"

"An incompetent one."

"So everything is still someone else's fault?" Mora pushed her.

But this time Stacy was prepared and held her ground and pushed back. "I said cut it out."

"AWS is not something to be ashamed of. It's a growing epidemic, but you don't have to stay its victim."

"AWS?"

"Angry Woman Syndrome. We're under more pressure than ever before and we're not handling it well. No, you don't have to be sugar and spice, but being a bitch isn't the only other option. You need to learn how to face life without letting it destroy you. But first you have to admit you want to change."

Stacy thought of Kelly's blog post, shouting at poor Houdini and ruining Chance's friend's car. "I do."

"Then punch this thing as hard as you can and tell me who or what it represents."

First she punched her ex--more than once. Then her brother, then her ex-housekeeper Kelly, then the woman at the prison--Laurice, the judge at her divorce trial, the officers who arrested her...soon she was punching away her feelings of inadequacy, fear of being alone, her sense of failure. She punched and then kicked the bag until her entire body trembled from exertion, sweat covering her. Then she threw off her gloves and screamed. "I don't want to be this way! I don't want to scare people. I want to be happy again. Every day I'm in pain. Every day hurts so much. I want things to be different!" She screamed again, until her voice was hoarse. Then she slid to the ground, brought her knees to her chest, lowered her head and sobbed. After a few moments she heard clapping. But not just one pair of hands, a group. Stacy heard applause. She cautiously lifted her head and saw the other woman from the group, cheering her.

Stacy hesitated wondering why they were smiling at her and wondering if the friendly gesture was a trick. Then she realized she didn't want to always be suspicious. She wanted to learn to trust again. She stood.

"Are you ready to take responsibility for your life?" Mora said coming forward.

"Yes."

She stood in front of Stacy and placed her hands on her hips."Life throws crap at all of us. Remember our stories aren't about our setbacks but our triumphs." She pointed to a petite woman, who looked like a former high school cheerleader. "Her ex sent her to the ER three times and still got custody of the kids." She pointed to another woman, tall elegant, dark skinned. "Her boss made sure she went down for an embezzlement scheme he committed. Do you know what separates the winners from the losers in life? It's not luck. It's how you respond to adversity. The losers give up and blame others. The winners take responsibility for their actions and focus on what they can control. The moment you can do that, the world is yours. So who's fault is it that your ex got alimony?"

Stacy's eyes widened. "You really want me to say that was my fault? He--"

"Had more friends than you. More influence than you. Why was that? Why did you let your friends disappear? Only one stayed. Where did the others go? Was it his fault?"

"No."

"Was it his fault that you decided to dedicate books to him he didn't help you write? Or that you gave up your dreams for him? Or that you buried yourself so that you could see him shine? You made a choice. He just exploited it. So again, I ask you, whose fault is it that your ex got alimony?"

Stacy gritted her teeth. "If I'd had a better lawyer."

Mora's gaze sharpened. "And whose fault is that? You chose him."

"I was stressed out and --"

"Stop making excuses." She jabbed Stacy's chest. "You chose a bad lawyer." She jabbed her again. "You chose a bad husband." And again. "You chose friends who dropped you when you needed them most. It's not about blame. It's about ownership. Everything in life has a cause and effect. If you drink poison and get sick, you can't blame the poison."

Stacy threw up her hands. "Fine. I admit I'm the biggest idiot in the world. And I deserve all that's happened to me."

Mora shook her head. "You're not an idiot, you're

human. And humans make mistakes. The moment you can admit that you've made some bad choices you can forgive yourself and start making right ones."

"Forgive myself?"

"Yes. Stacy, it's as simple as that. You can't trust others when you don't trust yourself. You have to believe in yourself again."

~

STACY RETURNED HOME FEELING good about herself, when her phone rang. "I've been waiting," her brother said after she answered.

Stacy gripped the phone then remembered all that she'd learned from anger management. She had to respond not react. She couldn't let him push her buttons. Stacy took a deep breath and checked Houdini's water bowl to make sure it was full then flopped down on the couch. "Why?"

"You said you'd call me back."

Stacy silently counted to ten. "Hmm."

"What's wrong with you? Did you hear what I said?"

"I spoke to Mom--"

"I told you not to tell them."

"I didn't. She called me and told me not to give you any money. So I'll say this once. You call me again with a lie like that and I'll turn you into my little sister. Understood?"

He swore. "Sorry, but I'm desperate. I just thought you might have a couple thousand."

"No."

"Not even a few hundred--"

Stacy kept her voice light. "Do you think I'm joking?"

"No," he said resigned. "But--"

"Bye," she said then hung up and grabbed Houdini's leash, feeling good that she didn't feel angry or upset but liberated. She was already a new woman and tomorrow she was going to the spa.

CHAPTER EIGHT

Dr. Michael Staton returned home after a long day at the hospital. He took off his tie and poured himself a drink. He then entered the bedroom and saw his wife lying on the ground, blood seeping from a wound on her forehead. He rushed over to her and cradled her in his arms. Then he raced to the phone and called an ambulance. In the mirror he saw a reflection of a dark figure outside the window. His heart started racing and his mouth wouldn't move. The room seemed to be closing in on him, but he couldn't let it over take him. He had to stay in control. She needed him. They all did. Everything depended on how he handled this moment. He turned and raced to the door and yanked on the handle. It fell into his hands.

"Cut!"

The woman on the ground burst into laughter. "That's the third doorknob you've broken."

Chance swallowed hard, wishing his heart rate would return to normal. He forced a smile. "I didn't break it."

The prop man immediately replaced the fixture. "I told you to be gentle."

"I'm a man in a hurry," Chance said with a hollow laugh, feeling a bead of sweat slide down his back. He took a deep breath and swallowed again, he wanted to run but he couldn't.

"Let's try again."

Those were words he didn't want to hear. He usually liked to get things done in one take, but he'd messed up and he had no one else to blame. He steadied his breathing and went through the second take feeling as if his body was moving in slow motion. He struggled to give the right looks, the right words but his brain was in a fog.

"Cut! Great job!"

He helped the lead actress, Samantha Huggins up. She looked at him. "Are you okay?"

"Fine as always."

They'd need to do reaction shots. He had to be prepared for them. "Give me a minute," he said hoping he didn't sound as breathless as he felt. He just needed air.

Chance went to his dressing room and washed his face, splashing the cold water to cool the burning sensation. You're not dying. He reminded himself. You're bigger than this. He didn't know why the panic attacks were getting more frequent. He had finally gotten what he wanted. Work as an actor. He enjoyed who he worked with. He couldn't let these attacks take that away from him. He wouldn't. No medication worked. Some made him too drowsy, others too hyper. He had an appointment with his doctor to start another prescription, but he was hesitant to go. He'd gotten the attacks to stop a few years back, he didn't know why they'd returned with a vengeance. He put drops in his eyes to wet his contact lens and took several deep, fortifying breaths. Soon he felt his heart beat slow. He would conquer this.

His cell phone rang and he absently glanced at the unfamiliar number then he did a double take: Stacy. He dashed for the phone and seized it forgetting his hands were wet. It slipped through his fingers and flew through the air. Fortunately, it landed on a chair. *Please don't hang up, please don't hang up.* He scrambled for it, drying his hands on his trousers, hitting his knee against a table and swearing before he grabbed the phone again. "Hello?"

"Are you okay? You sound out of breath."

Chance squeezed his eyes shut and rubbed his knee. "I'm fine."

"I just wanted to call and say hi."

God he'd missed hearing her voice. "I'm glad you did," he said trying not to sound too eager. *Cool. He had to stay cool.*

"I just completed Anger Management this week and soon I'll finish my class at the detention center," Stacy said sounding a little unsure.

"Congratulations."

"I guess what I'm trying to say is that although my time is busy right now, I hope to get to see you again." He heard her take a deep breath. "I've gotten a lot of things wrong in my life. And right now I have a lot I have to fix, but--"

To me you're perfect just the way you are. "Let me treat you to lunch this Saturday."

"You treated me last time."

"So? You choose the place." *Please say yes.*

"Okay."

"But I want you to be honest with me and tell me what you're dealing with."

"You don't want to know," she said.

"I wouldn't be asking if I didn't. Remember, I don't scare easily."

"Fine. I'll tell you, but I don't want you to feel obligated."

"You don't want me to care about my girlfriend and not try to help her? Of course I will."

"Girlfriend?" Stacy said, stumbling over the word.

"You want to be exclusive, right?"

"Yes, but--"

"I know it seems fast, but we're grownups and I don't think we need to pretend that we're not serious about each other."

"I didn't expect you to be so matter of fact about it," she said sounding happy.

"If I had the time I'd be over there right now and let you know how serious I am."

"And I wouldn't stop you," she said with a laugh.

Chance tugged on his collar feeling his temperature rise. He loved hearing her laugh. If he wasn't careful he'd start picturing her naked and imagining what he could do with her. He cleared his throat and fought to focus on what he had to say. "I want you to do something for me."

Stacy released a nervous laugh. "I'm afraid to ask. What do you want me to help you with?"

"I don't want you to help me with anything. I want you to accept me the way I am."

"I do."

He smiled. "You haven't seen my bad side yet. And there may be things you don't like about me, but I don't want you to use them against me." *Like the fact that I'm an actor.*

"I'm sure I can handle anything."

"Promise?"

"You're starting to sound really cryptic."

He rubbed his eyes. "I know and I don't mean to. The truth is--"

The sound of a doorbell cut through his words. "Oh damn," Stacy said. "I have to go. Tell me on Saturday. I promise I'll listen. Bye."

Chance disconnected and tapped his phone against his chin, hoping she'd keep her promise this time.

～

"Turn that crap off," Leon Paige said coming out of the shower annoyed to see his girlfriend watching *Heartbeat*. He had to see his brother next Sunday and didn't want to also have to see him on TV pretending to be a doctor when he was a real one.

"In a minute," she said waving him away. "Dr. Staton is about to discover the secret his wife's been hiding."

He sat down on the bed. "I said turn it off."

She sighed and put the TV on mute before saddling

his lap. "Had a hard day at work?" she said expertly getting his body to respond. Leon kissed her, in no mood to talk, but behind her head he still saw his brother's face on the TV. His older brother who'd left him to pick up the pieces of their broken family; forcing him to work night and day to get through college then medical school, achieving his mother's dream while his brother got fame and fortune without any of the sacrifice. Leon closed his eyes, letting his mind empty except for one last wish. He couldn't wait for the day when his brother's past would send him crashing down to earth.

CHAPTER NINE

HE WAS STILL INTERESTED. She'd been a little afraid he wouldn't be. Stacy knew new relationships could lose their passion fast. But if this was meant for the long term then she had nothing to worry about. He didn't care that she'd had to take anger management classes or her work at the jail. She already felt like a new woman and couldn't wait to see Chance again. *Her boyfriend.* Strangely it felt right. Everything about him felt that way. He was so easy to talk to and be around. Stacy wondered what he wanted to tell her. Why his tone suddenly sounded uneasy. She didn't want him to feel that way with her, but then what if it was a big secret? What if he was married? No, he didn't seem the type. Maybe he had a disease.

She shook her head. She had to stop thinking the worst. She'd let him tell her and then she'd know what to do

Stacy found her stomach full of butterflies thinking

of her hair appointment, although she looked forward to showing Chance her new look. She hadn't been to a hair salon in over five years. Although, she had taken the time to trim her ends, every six to eight weeks, she hadn't been consistent with doing deep conditioning and her hair looked the worst for it. She wasn't looking forward to receiving a lecture from someone who didn't know her and all that she'd been through.

She found the salon in a less fashionable part of the city and her hopes dimmed. She felt out of place. "He'll probably want to shave off one side of my head and color my hair purple!" she thought. She ascended a set of winding black iron stairs before she entered a golden ornate door that led into a wide open space, with a spectacular view.

"Hello, may I help you?" the receptionist asked. To Stacy's relief the young woman looked normal.

"Yes. I have an appointment with Damion."

The receptionist checked her schedule then frowned. "I'm sorry, but Damion doesn't have any appointment listed for today."

Stacy felt a rush of anger. "He'd better because I made one."

"I'm sorry, let me see if we have you listed on another day."

"I don't have another day," Stacy snapped. She took a deep breath, and got hold of her temper. It wasn't the receptionist's fault if things had been mixed up. "Please check the schedule again." She searched through her purse and then placed her Black Stockings membership card on the counter. "Maybe this will help."

The young woman's eyes widened. "Oh, I'm sorry. I didn't know you were one of them." The woman jumped to her feet and hurried around the counter. "Please don't tell anyone I messed up, but I just started here," she said taking Stacy's coat. She led Stacy to a private suite where a plush red robe and pair of slippers waited for her.

"Please get changed. Damion will be with you shortly."

Stacy put on the robe and slippers and looked around the small room, its large window offering another breathtaking view. On a small side table sat a cup of spicy chai tea. Stacy took a sip wondering if she was there for a haircut or lunch.

"There you are. Oh my, oh my, oh my..."

Stacy stared at the tall, wiry man. Faded acne marks marred his brown skin and he wore a light blue suit that seemed to shimmer in the light. He immediately started pulling at her hair. "This will all have to go. All of it."

Damion adjusted the chair, and raised her up so that he could get a better look. "They told me you'd neglected your hair, but honey, from what I see, you have all but killed it. You're lucky I can work miracles with almost anything." He walked around the chair looking at Stacy from different angles, she wasn't at all sure she liked being studied as if she were a specimen.

"To be honest with you, I had considered cutting it all off," she said.

"No. That wouldn't do. Your face needs shape. Just chopping off your hair, isn't the answer. You need to take off just enough. And I know exactly what will work." For the next hour, Damion clipped away, stepping back every now and then to admire his handy work, and when he was finished, he announced he was going to put in a 'cold wave'. "Your hair is perfect for the wave. It's coarse, but not too thick, and this way you can keep your short hair styled, very simply, while looking gorgeous at the same time, and not having to work too hard."

When Stacy got to see her new hair style, she was blown away. It was short, very short, but suited her. The sides were barely there, while he had allowed some length at the nape of her neck, and soft smooth waves on the top of her head. She looked chic, and felt like a million dollars. To add character to her hairstyle, he added soft purple and red highlights throughout, making her hair illuminate, depending on how the light hit each hair strand. Stacy looked and felt like someone totally different. Damion gave her a supply of hair products and instructed her to make sure to wash and condition frequently, plus get a regular trim to keep the hairstyle fresh and alive.

After her experience with Damion, Stacy felt ready for her appointment with Missy, the makeup artist. Missy looked as if she could be an extra in a sci-fi movie with her spiked blonde hair and extravagant make up. But she immediately put Stacy at ease with a quick smile. Several layers of cleansers and moisturizers later, Stacy had her brows shaped and eyelashes curled. Which was a first for her, at least by a professional. She had thick, heavy eyebrows but Missy shaped them, creating an amazing look.

Then Missy showed her a trick, using clear mascara to first coat the lashes, and how to use a specially designed eyelash curler, amazing Stacy at how much having her eyelashes curled opened up her eyes and made her entire face open up. As part of her final finish, Missy outlined Stacy's eyes with a smoky dark purple kohl eyeliner that made her dark brown pupils stand out. For her lips, Missy showed Stacy how to 'customize' her lip coloring, by adding just a small amount of foundation to vary the color slightly from the top to her bottom lip.

"You want your lip color to work for you, not against you. You want whatever color you select to emphasize your mouth and what it stands for. Your lips need to compliment your face, and draw attention to who you are, and what you are about. Take the time to select the colors that work for you and your skin tone, and of course, to match or work with the colors you plan to wear, and you will be amazed.

"I can tell you're the type of person that doesn't go for the perfectly flawless look, so you don't have to use a foundation all over your face. Just in certain spots." Next Missy showed Stacy how to apply foundation, only on her cheeks and the middle of her forehead, and blend it evenly with the rest of her skin tone, for a natural look. Stacy looked stunning. Before she left, Missy handed Stacy a small collection of brightly colored eye shadows, "Now, whenever you are feeling just a little adventurous, or want to 'spruce' up your look, just use one or more of these, they are excellent for making your eyes standout, and you will get the attention you want."

Stacy grinned. Right now, she only cared about getting one man's attention.

CHAPTER TEN

"Oh wow!" Julia said when she opened the door. Stacy wanted her friend to be the first one to see her makeover. She had driven to Julia's gated community and had checked her hair one more time before ringing the doorbell to her friend's exclusive brownstone. Julia stared at her. "You look amazing." It had been a couple of weeks since she'd last seen her.

"Getting rid of an ex will do that," Stacy said stepping inside. She followed Julia to the kitchen and heard the TV where Julia's seventeen-year-old daughter, Emily, sat in the family room.

Julia hugged her friend. "What happened?"

"I've finally got a life and I've met someone. We're meeting again soon."

Julia took Stacy's coat and hung it in the closet. "And you thought you'd never find love again."

"I didn't say anything about love. But he's great. I'm taking things slow," she said although in truth she wanted to speed things up. She couldn't wait to see Chance again.

Don't do this to me, she heard Chance say. Stacy froze surprised by how real and close his voice seemed. Like an auditory hallucination.

Julia looked at her concerned. "What is it?"

Stacy shook her head feeling foolish. Her face growing warm. She had to get herself together. "Nothing. I thought I heard---it's nothing." But it wasn't nothing when she heard his voice again. It was as if he was in the next room. His tone distinctive, but this time casual, amused. Stacy left the kitchen and followed the sound to the family room, but of course he wasn't there. Emily sat focused on the TV screen. Stacy was about to turn away when she heard his voice again then saw his face appear.

Stacy stared at the TV, a sudden coldness settling in the pit of her stomach. What was Chance doing on TV? Why was his face staring back at her on the screen? But it wasn't the Chance she remembered. It wasn't the man with a shabby beard and casual clothes. This man was clean shaven and gorgeous. Part of her didn't want it to be him, maybe it was a lookalike. But she couldn't deny that mouth, those eyes, and the voice. They were all distinctly his. She swallowed.

"What's wrong?" Julia said behind her holding a plate filled with an assortment of party crackers and several cheese slices.

"He's an actor," she said as if he were fatally ill.

"They're all actors. Did you think this was a reality TV show or something?"

Emily looked away from the screen. "Oh, you look great."

Stacy forced a smile, no longer caring what she looked like. "Umm...what show are you watching?"

"*Heartbeat.*"

"And the actor's name is Chance Jamison?" she asked just to make sure. She wanted to be wrong.

"Yes, he's really good," Emily said. "He's been on the show for six years. He's Dr. Michael Staton. His father is a total jerk and his brother is sleeping with his wife, but he doesn't know it yet. He's so sweet. He's really in love with Monica Young but he had to marry Nicole in order to save the family medical practice, but she's also just using him."

"I see," Stacy said, although she wasn't interested.

"Juicy entertainment," Julia said adding a pitcher of lemonade to the refreshments.

Stacy turned from the screen no longer able to face the truth. He was an actor. She'd almost fallen for another actor. "I have to leave."

"Why?" Julia said alarmed. "Tell me what's wrong?"

"I have to go."

"Not until you tell me what's going on."

"I went out with him."

"Who?"

"Chance Jamison," Stacy said in a breathless rush.

"What?"

Why hadn't he told her he was an actor? She inwardly groaned remembering all the awful things she'd said about those in his profession. "I can't believe he's an actor," she said her voice cracking.

"And he's gorgeous," Julia added. "You have to break it off with him."

Stacy stared at her friend confused. "What?"

"You cannot keep seeing him. You've got to break this pattern. Actors are your weakness. You just got rid of Marshall."

"He's not Marshall."

"You're rebounding."

"After three years? I haven't dated in--"

"Exactly. You're picking the first guy who shows interest in you. That's not healthy. I let you talk me out of going to court with you, although I knew I shouldn't have, and I kept my mouth shut when you were married. Now listen to me. You need to stay away from actors. You need to find a man who will adore you. A man like that," she pointed to Chance's image, "is surrounded by beautiful temptations. You don't want to have to compete with that."

Stacy's cell phone rang and she saw his number.

"Is that him?" Julia asked.

"Yes, he's taking me to lunch this weekend."

"Cancel."

"But I--"

"If you can't talk to him then let the phone ring. Trust me. I'm looking out for you."

Stacy sighed, feeling uncertain. She knew her friend cared but this felt wrong. When the phone stopped ringing she felt her heart drop.

Julia took the phone from Stacy and grinned. "Good, he got the message." Her smile disappeared when a text appeared on the screen.

"What does it say?" Stacy asked.

"He's just telling you where he's taking you," Julia said swiftly texting back a reply. "Don't worry I'll handle this for you."

"What are you doing?"

"I'm canceling as we agreed."

Stacy snatched the phone back before Julia could text something else when she looked down she saw he'd said

R U OK?

"Tell him you're fine," Julia said peering over her shoulder.

Stacy bit her lip then wrote: Raincheck?

Sure.

Julia shook her head. "You shouldn't have said that, but it's a start." She beamed at Stacy. "You won't regret this. With the way you look now you'll have no problem meeting plenty of men. You'll forget all about Chance."

Stacy plastered on a smile, gripping the phone in her hand, forcing herself not to text him back and tell him it was all a mistake. Was Julia right? Were actors really her weakness? Was she repeating a bad pattern?

At home Stacy sat in her living room and stared at her cell phone. Houdini kept bringing her toys for her to play with him, but she wasn't in the mood so he finally settled at her feet. She absently stroked him. Her life with Marshall had been a rollercoaster and she now wanted some stability. Part of her felt that he was someone she could trust and depend on. Or was that just a fantasy? Julia was right, she wouldn't be able to compete with the glamorous women in his life and she shouldn't fall for the first man she met after getting a divorce.

She was now part of the Black Stockings Society. She wasn't going to be the woman she'd been in the past. Maybe she'd been too quick to settle for him. She was going to meet someone new. She sent Chance one last text message positive she'd never see him again.

~

LET'S BE FRIENDS.

Chance reread the message several times, just to make sure. What did she mean by that? What happened? She'd cancelled their date, but had said yes to a rain check. What was going on? He replied to her text, but received no reply and his phone calls got the same response.

She was pushing him out of her life. He'd allowed that once, but he wasn't going to let her do it a second time.

CHAPTER ELEVEN

THIS WASN'T GOING to work. Stacy stared at the two-piece outfit she'd selected to go with her new pair of stockings for the next day. Why would they ask her to wear silk hose to her third week of class at the detention center? The women still didn't respect her and she doubted this would help her cause. The only attention she'd get would be from the male guards. Houdini barked and a second later she found out why, when someone knocked on the door.

Who could be visiting her? Had Chance decided to reply to her text in person? Stacy looked through the peephole, but couldn't see anything. She braced herself then opened the door. An attractive, full figured, impeccably groomed black woman, her thick hair in one long braid wrapped to frame her face, stood there. "I'm sure he'll come next time." The woman entered and walked ahead of Stacy, her collection of gold bracelets tinkling against each other, while her large hooped earrings swung from side to side.

Stacy stood dumbfounded. "Who will come? And you are...?"

"I apologize," she said holding out her hand. "I'm Rania with the Black Stockings Society." She slowly looked Stacy up and down. "Is that what you plan to wear tomorrow?"

"Yes."

Rania shook her head. "No, that will not do."

"I'm going to teach my class at the detention center, not attend a fashion show."

"And, how are the classes going?" Rania asked taking a seat.

"Well, I was having problems getting several of the women to uhm, listen. Now that I've completed my anger management course I'm sure I can accomplish anything."

"I don't need you to sound like a presenter at a motivational course," Rania said with a laugh. "You want to command respect from those women and it starts with your closet."

"My closet?"

"Yes. It's all about the way you dress."

Stacy glanced down at her outfit. "What's the matter with the way I dress? It's the stockings that are wrong."

"The stockings are fine. However, what you're wearing says nothing about you. You sound like you still want to start a fight."

Stacy made a face, insulted. "No, I don't. I've changed."

"Then stop wearing clothes that say, in large letters I may add," Rania swept her hand through the air as though reading a banner. "I don't think much of myself, I'm a wimp, please step all over me, I don't matter. Now show me to your closet."

Moments later, Rania rummaged through the items hanging in Stacy's closet then sniffed. She picked up a faded black top. "This says 'kick me'." She tossed it on the bed. She held up a pair of sweatpants. "This says 'I'm pathetic'." She picked up another item. "This says 'I have no figure'. And this." She tossed the shapeless top on the floor. "I can't even repeat what this says."

Stacy watched in amazement as Rania emptied out her closet. After years of put downs by Marshall, Stacy knew she'd let herself go, but she'd never realized how much. When had her wardrobe become so boring and colorless? When the doorbell rang, Rania told her to wait then left the room. Moments later she returned with two men carrying an assortment of stylish clothes from skirts and dresses to silk tops and sleek jackets. "Put them in there." She directed.

Stacy stared speechless. "What is all this?"

"Your new wardrobe."

"But--"

"We don't have time to argue right now, we'll go through the items later, but for tomorrow, I have a specific outfit in mind."

Minutes later, Stacy looked at herself in the mirror. She looked...stunning. No, more than that...distinguished in a tailored white shirt, with a fitted, dark green, knee-high pencil skirt. It had a side slit that revealed her long legs and showed off her thigh-high laced dark-blue decorative stockings and three-inch black suede shoes. Not only did she look impressive, she felt totally different. She even walked differently.

Stacy put on the sunglasses Rania handed her. She couldn't wait until the women saw her at the center. "Ladies, look out."

$\sim$

THE MOMENT she stepped out of her car and walked across the parking lot, Stacy knew things would be different. All heads turned to look at her, she just stared ahead. As she passed through security, the guards were unable to concentrate on what they were doing, she didn't notice them. She made sure she arrived at least twenty minutes earlier, so that she was already set up before the women entered the classroom. As the women piled in, their chatter stilled until there was not a sound to be heard. They took their seats, amazed by the transformation in their teacher.

"So, are you going to a party or something?" Laurice said.

Stacy made no attempt to reply. She stood and adjusted her skirt, showing off her stealth figure.

"Starting today, if you don't want to be in my class, you can request to be removed. I've already spoken to the Warden. Secondly, if I give you an assignment, I expect it to be done, if not, you're out. Thirdly, if you have a problem with me and my teaching style, too bad, I'm all you've got. Once again, you can ask to be transferred to another program. Do I make myself clear?"

Three women got up and left, to Stacy's surprise the queen stayed. She wondered if it was a challenge, but didn't want to overanalyze.

Not only had her demeanor changed, but her 'don't mess with me' attitude totally caught them off guard. As for the correctional officer, he couldn't take his eyes off of her, not that she wanted any more of his attention. For the next two hours Stacy had total command of her class, she felt on top of the world, and didn't plan on taking the pair of stockings off anytime soon. After running several errands, she went grocery shopping, picked up her dry cleaning, and stopped at the pet store to pick up some of Houdini's favorite treats. Everywhere she went, it was as if people parted to make way for her, she felt exhilarated, that was until she saw a picture of Chance on the front of a magazine.

Everything went downhill from there. The moment she stepped through the front door, Houdini made a mad dash to greet her, as did the two other dogs her new dog sitter had brought with her. The sitter apologized profusely, trying to rein in the dogs each one jumping on Stacy, their tails wagging furiously and with each jump their claws ripping her stockings, creating a series of massive runs. Finally, the dog sitter was able to settle the pack down and left.

Tears filled Stacy's eyes, what an end to a perfect day--ripped stockings, she'd have to search for a new sitter *and* she had a broken heart. Getting over Chance wasn't as easy as Julia said it would be. She grabbed a sofa pillow and screamed into it. Houdini, sensing something wrong, hid behind the couch. After several minutes, Stacy tossed the pillow down, feeling more in control of her temper and found Houdini sound asleep behind the couch. She didn't bother to change and decided to take out the trash. She froze when she saw Chance coming down the hall. She had no place to hide. He looked like the man on the TV come to life. He looked tough, lean and sexy. She held out her hand. "Stop right there."

He kept walking.

She turned, ran back into her apartment and closed the door. She caught a glimpse of her reflection in the mirror. She looked like a sad clown with her red nose and smudged mascara.

The doorbell rang.

Stacy briefly shut her eyes.

The doorbell rang again.

She swore and opened her eyes.

The doorbell rang again more insistent. Houdini ran to the door, his tail wagging in anticipation. "Not now boy." She gently took his collar and led him to her office and closed the door.

Stacy sighed then opened the front door and glared at him. "Why do you always show up when I'm at my absolute worse? Why couldn't you have shown up this morning? I looked amazing then, but *nooo* you had to come now when my mascara is ruined, my stockings are torn and..." Her voice died away, subdued by the power of his dark gaze, which held her captive. His dark brown eyes, usually so easy going and carefree, blazed with an emotion she'd never seen before. A hungry emotion that made her skin tingle and caused her to forget how awful she looked.

"I'm not interested in just being friends," Chance said in a low, silky tone.

Stacy paused puzzled by his calm statement. "You came all the way over here to tell me that?"

He nodded, but didn't move.

"I just don't think it's fair to--"

He folded his arms. "When did you find out?"

"What?"

"That I'm an actor. That's what changed your mind, right?"

"I didn't change my mind I just--"

"You broke your promise. I asked you to accept me the same way I accept you."

Stacy shook her head feeling miserable. "It's not that simple."

Chance stopped her with a kiss that sent her stomach into a whirl. When he drew away raw hurt reflected in his gaze. "I can't believe you still don't..." He let his words fade away.

"Don't what?"

He shook his head. "Doesn't matter anymore. I thought it did. You're going to miss me. When you want to stop playing games, you know how to reach me." He turned to leave.

Stacy reached out to him, then gripped her hand into a fist. "I'm not playing games. I just need--" she stopped.

"You need what?" he asked, keeping his back to her.

To make sure I'm not making the same mistake twice. It was tempting to confide in him, to say the words that would make him turn around, but she knew she couldn't. Not yet. Not until she was a success again. Not until she knew she wouldn't become dependent on him. Not until she was certain she wouldn't get her heart broken.

Chance nodded and sighed, her silence giving him the answer he didn't want to face. "Bye Stacy," he said, then walked away.

≈

A WEEK LATER, Stacy tried to convince herself that letting Chance go was for the best, although she knew it was a lie. He was right. She missed him while walking and playing with Houdini, while watching TV, while sleeping at night. She looked forward to her writing class so that she had something to do other than think about him. She sat at the desk looking at the last assignment she'd given them and knew the women wouldn't like what she had to say.

"Thank you all for working so hard on your home-work. It was a very fascinating read. Well written, excit-ing, engaging. I was really impressed. And there were two things that impressed me. First, what you submitted was remarkably similar to a story I read five years ago; second, half of you turned in the same story. Laziness I can accept." She clasped her hands. "And I understand that for a number of you, stealing doesn't matter, but it does to me. You don't have to care about being here, but I do expect you to be woman enough to own your own words and work."

"I didn't steal nothing," Laurice said.

"Okay, then tell me why you chose to have a white Connecticut socialite as the main character."

"Because I wanted to."

Stacy shook her head. "Try again."

"I don't have to explain nothing to you."

"No, and you don't have to be here either."

"Look, we're sorry," another woman said.

Laurice raised her voice. "Don't be apologizing for me."

"We don't want to get in trouble," Priscilla said.

"I didn't do nothing."

"How did you know?" Priscilla asked.

"How did I know what?" Stacy asked.

"That we didn't write it?"

"Every writer has a voice. You can't hear it but readers can. I didn't hear your voice on the page. Sometimes you can mimic another writer's voice, but that's different from plagiarizing, which is stealing someone else's story and saying it's your own. Courageous people know how to take a plot and make it their own."

Priscilla shook her head. "But I don't know any good stories."

"You like music, right?"

"Yes."

"Tell me about your favorite song."

"It's a rap."

"And?"

"It's about this guy who's tired of living on the streets and dreams of something more."

"That's the plot right there."

"What do you mean?"

"Okay, here's another assignment. I want you all to take that song as your premise."

"What?"

"Premise is...never mind. Write a story about a guy who has dreams he wants to reach. Give him a goal and end it with him either getting it or not."

"How old should he be?" one woman asked.

"Doesn't matter."

"Can I give him my brother's name?" another asked.

"Whatever you want."

"Can I--"

Stacy waved her hands. "There are no rules. You are the puppet master, you are the god in your writing universe. You tell me whatever story you want."

"Thanks for giving us another chance," Priscilla said before leaving.

"I didn't do nothing wrong," Laurice said as she left the room.

They all left. The guard stayed behind. "You know, trying to teach these women morals is a waste of breath. They're here because they have none."

"They can learn. Once they're out--"

"They'll end up right back here. Most do."

~

She'd told her students that the assignment had no rules. Maybe she could start writing again. Stacy thought for a moment. She could give herself an assignment so that she could completely forget Marshall and Chance. She didn't want to admit how much she missed Chance. How could one brief encounter mean so much? Was it because she was lonely and had started living again? She needed to be challenged. An assignment would force her to face her fears and close the past forever. She bit her lip and paced. She was afraid. Afraid she didn't have it anymore. That she was all dried up. But maybe...

Stacy sat down in front of her laptop and started writing. Strangely, what she wrote quickly became semiautobiographical. She'd expected to write another novel, a novel didn't need anyone else--but found herself writing a screenplay. A script needed actors and more to make it come alive. But that didn't bother her. Writing felt cathartic. To write about a world she knew, that had made and betrayed her, starring a man who was nothing but illusions and the woman who'd allowed herself to be deluded by them. She wrote in a white heat for the rest of the week then sent the finished manuscript to Julia, but the moment she did she regretted her action. It wasn't polished. She'd let her heart bleed on the page. What if Julia hated it? Did it matter? It was done. She'd written again, when she never thought she would.

Stacy got on her treadmill and started listening to a new audio book from her favorite mystery author. She liked the delivery, but for some reason the voice felt more intimate this time. It was as if she knew the narrator. She loved the story about a rugged PI, but the actor's delivery had something special about it. Familiar. She picked up the digital music player and looked at the name of the narrator. "Chance Jamison." She stopped the recording. Chance again? One moment she hardly knew the man and now he was everywhere. Even in her bedroom. She wouldn't listen to it anymore, she'd just read the book. She went into the living room and decided to stream some movies instead, and as she searched the selection she saw his show. She selected the first season, telling herself she just wanted to see what had people talking. Why her friend's daughter was hooked, what made the series work. It was all for research. Before she knew it, she was in the throes of a TV binge and lost an entire weekend.

And like a person with a hangover, she felt miserable the following day. She was disgusted with her weakness. She wanted to forget him. She didn't want to be one of the millions of women who fawned over him. She went to sleep that night and found herself in a hospital bed and Dr. Michael Staton was the attending physician and he healed her in ways that left her hungry for more. Stacy woke up feeling aroused and annoyed. She called Julia and asked her to go for a jog. After a halfhearted effort they stopped at a nearby deli and chatted. Someone had left a magazine behind. Stacy idly flipped through the magazine then saw Chance's face.

He really did have a nice face. She knew it was even better in person. She traced his eyebrows and his mouth. His beautiful, wonderful mouth. She remembered how his lips felt against hers.

Julia snatched the magazine away and snapped it shut. "I've got a guy for you."

"I'm not interested."

"You have to do something to get over him."

"I *am* over him," Stacy said taking a bite of her poppy seed bagel.

"You were drooling over his picture."

"I was admiring the digital artistry."

"I can't believe you were able to say that with a straight face. You are looking so good lately and wasting your time on something's that's over. Where did you get that track suit?"

"From...umm...a friend."

"You don't have any friends beside me."

"Oh, thanks."

"It's true. Come on. What's your secret to suddenly looking so good?"

"No secret, I just went on a buying binge--retail therapy." She knew she couldn't tell Julia about her new wardrobe courtesy of the Black Stockings Society.

"It's just that, even when I first met you, you didn't look this good."

"A divorce changes you. It might take time for my heart to heal, but nothing stops me from looking good now."

Julia clapped her hands together. "Speaking of time. I got your email. I'll get back to you soon."

"Forget it. I just went crazy for a week. Delete it."

But Julia didn't delete it. A week later as Stacy was putting Houdini in the back seat of her car after a vet appointment her cell phone rang.

"How much do you want?" Julia said without preamble.

"How much for what?"

"Don't be coy. You knew I'd love it. I can't believe you've been hiding this from me. I know you fired your last agent. You're working with a lawyer now right? Just give me a round number and I'll--"

"What are you talking about?"

"The script you sent me. It's just what I've been looking for. I already have a major studio exec chomping at the bits to get the exclusive rights to air it."

"My script. You liked my script?"

"I loved it. If you had any doubt that you needed Marshall, this script proves you don't. He's gonna hate you, and that makes me want to produce it that much more. Any money woes are over, I hope you're working on something else. You're on a streak and I don't think it's gonna stop. I'll call and hash things out, then I'll tell you about all that we're going to do. I'm so glad you're trusting me with this. You haven't shown this to anyone else, right?"

"No, of course not."

"That's my girl. Talk to you soon."

Stacy put her phone away. Julia liked her script and wanted to produce it. She hadn't written a script in years, not since her separation, and Julia thought it was wonderful. Stunned, Stacy got in the driver's seat and put the keys in the ignition.

CHAPTER TWELVE

"I KNOW a script that has your name on it," Tyson said coming into Chance's dressing room. "It has a part I know you're perfect for, although no one thinks you have a chance of getting it."

Chance turned a page of the magazine he was skimming and didn't look up as Tyson settled into a chair. "Nice to see you too."

"Aren't you going to ask me what it is?"

"No."

"*Courting Danger*, Stacy Price's comeback piece. It's rumored the script is loosely based on her rocky marriage to Marshall Price. Buzz is already going around about the producer, Julia Jones, and director, Donald Mott, who's attached to the project. Every actor I know wants a piece of the action. Everyone's guessing who's going to play the lead role of, Melvin, Marshall's character." He slammed the script down on the table with a dramatic flourish.

Chance fought to remain neutral, although the sound

of Stacy's name still brought pain. It had been two months since he'd last seen her and he wondered if he'd made the right decision. "Sounds like a great part," he said acting the role of man who didn't care, although he cared more than he wanted to.

"Which is why you should play it."

Chance sniffed. "I don't think I was one of the names mentioned."

"That's because they don't know you're interested yet."

"I didn't say I was. Besides, I'm the nice guy, the cool, good guy. Do you really think I can play a charming snake?"

"I know you can. You can play anything you want to." He tapped the script. "This role is meant for you."

Chance picked up the script, just to humor his friend. He wasn't really interested in vying for a role that a lot of other actors wanted. Especially a role written by a woman who'd turned his world upside down. He didn't want to have anything to do with her. No, that was wrong, he wanted to do a lot with her--in a very personal way. Since Tyson looked so eager, Chance skimmed through a couple of pages and quickly became riveted. He swore. The role was good and he wanted it. He wanted a role to stretch his skills. He was bored playing the good looking hero. He wanted to cut his teeth on a nice juicy villain. But it wasn't just the role that capti-vated him, it was the script, the language, the passion in every line. He knew he could add a lot of dimension to this character.

Chance knew most wouldn't think he would be right

for the part, because he made playing Dr. Staton look easy. What most people didn't know was that he could mold his movements to suit any part he played. While some actors melded themselves into the roles they played, he could shed a character as easily as taking off a coat. He never confused himself with who he was and the people he played. Unlike Dr. Staton, he hadn't grown up surrounded by the privileges of wealth. He had a decent lower, middle class background, raised by a single immigrant woman and his Gran. The stage had called to him the moment he recited Jonah and the Whale in church. The applause had lingered. He discovered he could make his mother smile, when smiles had been few in his home. He saw how his mother and grandmother escaped into the TV and how those characters on the screen made them smile and he wanted to do the same. He wanted to entertain. To let people live a different life, if only for a while. His mother and grandmother hadn't been too thrilled with his ambitions.

They'd hoped he'd want to become a professor or doctor, but he'd chosen the stage instead, leaving for the bright lights and big promises of New York the moment he graduated high school. Because of his looks, he hadn't had to wait around long, getting modeling jobs, and bit parts in off Broadway shows and small roles in indie films, before landing a spot in a national commercial that paid the bills. That was before he landed the role on *Heartbeat*, which he'd played for the last six years. But Chance was hesitant. If he went after this new role, he knew it would be more pressure and he couldn't afford to let his panic attacks be seen.

Chance put the script down, tapping down his eagerness too. "It was a nice thought."

Tyson pushed the script back at him. "It's not like you to be chicken."

"I just don't want you to be disappointed."

"I thought you'd eat up an opportunity like this."

Chance sighed. "They're back."

Tyson paused then swore. "Really?"

He nodded. Tyson had been one of the few people he'd felt safe enough to share with about his attacks.

"I know another doctor."

"I'm already seeing another one this week."

"It's your family, isn't it?"

Yes. His family life had been one reason he liked the world of make-believe. Since he'd been a boy he'd wanted to escape it. But no matter how hard he tried they kept pulling him back to the realities of his life. He glanced at a picture his ten year old niece, Tiffany, had given him. She was the one bright spot in his life. Unfortunately, her welfare was also his greatest concern. He'd recently had a talk with his lawyer about possibly having to fight his brother about his sister's care--Tiffany's mother. His sister's mental status affected his niece and worried him. "I don't know what it is, I just know that they hit me at the worst moments. Could you see me going for this audition, and then freaking out?" he said, not wanting to go into detail about his family.

"You don't freak out and this is the opportunity you've been waiting for." Tyson stood and held Chance's shoulders. "I don't care what medication you have to take, what therapy you have to do. Make this happen. It's going to be stressful and cutthroat, but you didn't get into this game expecting it to be easy. You can do this. You've worked hard for a moment like this. And with the contract you have with *Heartbeat* you can be flexible with your shooting schedule."

"Hmm," Chance said being noncommittal. He knew that they'd be able to write around his character on *Heartbeat* for several weeks. But it'd still be a grueling schedule carrying two projects. But the thought of eighteen hour days only invigorated him.

"I've already dropped your name with a few key people. Make me proud."

Chance smiled and slumped back in his chair. "Forget it."

Tyson sighed. "Let's go for a drink this weekend."

"Can't. I'm attending a fundraiser."

"Another one? What's this one for? Save the butterflies?"

"Very funny. It's for mental health research."

Tyson sobered knowing that the subject was close to Chance's heart. "Oh."

Before Tyson could say anything else, Tameka Hart, an aspiring actress with a curvy figure and pretty eyes, burst into his dressing room. "Are we still on for Saturday? You won't believe who's going to be there. Julia Jones." She leaned over and kissed him. "You'll love my dress."

Chance winked. "I know I will."

She giggled then left.

Tyson frowned. "I thought you were going to dump her."

"I did. Months ago. We're just friends."

"Who kiss like lovers?"

He sighed. "She came to me crying her eyes out over a bad audition--"

"That's because she can't act."

"She's getting better."

"She has as much acting ability as a tube of tooth-paste. At least you can squeeze something good out of one. She's got nothing but a pretty face and a delusion. She's hanging onto you because she knows you're better than she is. I've seen it lots of times. Find your action in another direction."

"I'm not sleeping with her."

"If she has her way you will be."

"When I go to parties and other events, she saves me from getting trapped by women and I help her get noticed. It works for both of us."

"Do you know what your problem is? You're too nice," Tyson said before Chance could reply. "You're taking your character Dr. Staton with you into the real world."

"No, I'm not like him."

Tyson patted Chance on the back. "Good, then go for this role. If Julia Jones or anyone related to her is at this fundraiser let them know who you are."

"Right," Chance said knowing he'd do no such thing.

Once Tyson had gone, Chance paced. *You can do this. You can do this. That role could be yours.* He grabbed his shirt, wishing the room didn't feel so hot. He didn't know what affected him more, the thought of trying for a role that few others believed he could do or the possibility of seeing Stacy again. The woman who hadn't known who he was. Who'd treated him like a regular guy. Then changed when she found out the truth. He wished he could be a regular guy.

Tyson came back into the room. "Do you know what your problem is?"

Chance covered his eyes and shook his head. "Just tell me."

"You're letting a woman stand in your way."

"What?"

"You didn't like when I mentioned Stacy's name. There's something you're not telling me, but I know that look. Don't pass up this opportunity because of revenge."

"Revenge?"

"I know she's the one who messed up my car. I don't want you to think that you are at a disadvantage because of what happened with the court case."

"I'm not going after the role."

"You will."

Chance couldn't help a smile. No, he wasn't going to audition for the role, but his friend had just given him an idea.

∿

THE LAST DAY of class had come faster than expected. Stacy was surprised to realize that she didn't want it to end. She'd finally felt she was making progress and now it was over. Now she could go back to her normal life and never see this place again. Ninety days. In three months spring had turned into summer, she'd met a man, lost that man, made enemies, made new friends, and started to write again. The experience had changed her, the women had too. They'd shown her where making the right choices could lead her.

"Where's Laurice?"

"Released."

Stacy had wanted to say goodbye. Laurice had been a challenge. Stacy still didn't know why she stayed, or why she made every meeting a fight, but her work had improved and they'd settled into a civility Stacy had grown used to. Stacy had wanted to tell her that her last story had been amazing. Coarse, and a little crude, but it was heartfelt and real. She had a talent with words, but now Laurice had already moved on.

The women said their goodbyes. There were a few tears. Priscilla asked if she could write her, but although Stacy said yes, she doubted she would. Even Nila had moved on from the puppy program. She'd left shortly after Stacy had met her, leaving someone else in charge and no forwarding address.

Stacy heard the jail door click close one last time, this time behind her instead of in front of her and walked out of the detention center closing one chapter and ready for the next.

∾

BUT STACY WASN'T sure how ready she was when she looked at the stockings she was supposed to wear to her next function. Rania had called and told her what to wear, but she wouldn't wear them. She *couldn't* wear them. She'd heard of black fishnets, even red ones. But purple? How could she pull off wearing a pair of purple fishnet stockings to a high-class fundraiser? Maybe there had been a mix up. She shouldn't have joined this club. Maybe she wasn't ready for it. Besides, she hadn't met anyone yet, except for Chance and he didn't count. If she didn't wear it no one would know, right?

Ready to live dangerously? Yes, she was, but did it have to be this dangerous? She liked to blend in. Besides, she wasn't supposed to be the star of the evening, the charity was. She knew there would be a lot of actors and actresses vying for attention while also elevating a worthy cause. They would try to charm and flatter her, so that they could be part of the film. Stacy took a deep breath. *I can do this.* She carefully did her makeup and hair, put on a backless, silver dress Rania had selected and then the stockings then stared at what she saw, hardly recognizing herself.

"Do you really think I can pull this off?" she said to Houdini who lay next to her bed. She bit her lip. "We'll find out," she said slipping on her heels.

The moment she entered the ballroom she got her answer. While she marveled at the opulent surroundings with its vaulted ceilings, large windows and black and white tile floors and imported glass vases bursting with large bouquets, others did a double take. Julia rushed up to her, fashionably attired in a classic black dress and diamond stud earrings. "I didn't even recognize you at first. You look sensational. You've got to tell me where you got that dress and those stockings."

"I will, when I remember."

Julia lifted a brow. "Keeping secrets?"

"Just a few." Stacy pulled out her cell phone and stylus and started writing down notes.

"What are you doing?"

"I have to keep busy," Stacy said. She hadn't been to a party in so long she felt out of touch.

"There are plenty of men here who'd love to keep you busy."

"That's not why I'm here."

"Consider it a bonus. Relax. Just have several drinks and smile and let them do the rest."

Stacy waved her friend away. "You go and do that. I'm already working on ideas for my next screenplay."

"Oh, I like the sound of that. Don't let me bother you." She leaned in close. "Just remember, Mr. Right could be here."

Stacy watched Julia join another conversation. She still hadn't forgotten about Chance. Why did Mr. Wrong still seem so right? Stacy shook her head, annoyed with her thoughts and jotted down a possible scene when a man bumped her elbow and her stylus slipped through her fingers and dropped to the ground. She bent to pick it up when someone absently kicked it out of reach. She made her way through the crowd, but people kept kicking it in various directions. Finally it hit a man's shoe and she hoped he'd stay still long enough for her to reach it.

≈

CHANCE GLANCED down when he felt something hit his shoe, and saw a stylus. He bent down to pick it up then stopped when he saw a pair of shiny black heels come into view. He slowly lifted his gaze and saw a pair of legs that made his mouth go dry. Chance would not have considered himself a leg man until that night. If he were truly honest he liked hips. Not that he'd admit that to anyone. But when he saw those smooth brown legs in purple fishnet stockings he was mesmerized. He finally raised his gaze to the form fitting silver dress and grew eager to see the owner of both. He grinned, but when he saw her face, his smile froze in place.

CHAPTER THIRTEEN

"THANK YOU," Stacy said in a stiff voice.

Chance handed over the stylus, not knowing what else to say. His tongue felt heavy in his mouth, his throat dry as he stared at a woman so stunning that everything else faded away. The lights could not rival the sparkle in her eyes, the flowers could not compare to the scent of her perfume. He wanted her and hated her at the same time. This wasn't the woman he'd been angry with, the woman who'd smashed his car, who he had found crying in the men's room, who he'd kissed with mascara running down her cheeks or who'd asked him to 'just be friends'. This was a woman without weakness. She carried herself like a member of a monarchy, her stance had an imperial bearing as if she could easily crush a man under her heels or slice him with a glance. This was a woman of power who didn't need anyone--especially him. With one glance she could send him soaring into heaven then crashing down to Earth.

Chance felt anger rising, hating how much she affected him. She was as tempting as a jet to a man who liked speed, a rainstorm to a parched desert. Everything about her was just right for him. He wanted to taste her raspberry colored lips, discover what was under her dress and spend a night with her. He hated that he still cared that she didn't remember him and that he wanted her to. He wanted to see a spark of recognition in her eyes. But all he saw was awkward surprise. This wasn't the Stacy he'd been thinking about. This wasn't the woman he'd been planning to coerce. She was the beauty he'd expected her to become, but just as she'd ignored his feelings in the past he knew she would again. She was a stranger to him now and it wounded his ego, but strengthened his resolve. She'd forgotten him and he'd do the same. He turned and took a glass from a passing waiter.

"You're right," she said in a soft voice. "I miss you."

Chance took a long swallow then gritted his teeth. He hadn't expected her to say that and she sounded sincere. He felt himself weakening, although he fought to keep an emotional distance. Chance steeled himself against her words, against his desire to forgive her and admit that he wanted to be with her, that he wanted to stand closer to her so that he could feel her soft, supple skin against his.

Stacy lightly touched his sleeve. "I made a mistake and I have to say this fast before Julia sees me and thinks I've lost my mind. Can I call you?"

Chance opened his mouth to respond, but before he could someone grabbed his face and kissed him full on the mouth. It was only when she pulled back he recognized it was his date. "Baby I've missed you." She turned to Stacy and held out her hand. "I'm Tameka Hart."

Stacy shook her hand. "Stacy Price."

"Do you mind if I steal him away for a minute?" Tameka said taking his arm. "There's someone you have to meet."

"No, I don't," Chance said quickly, trying to get over the kiss and the look on Stacy's face.

"No, please," Stacy said, taking a step back. "Go ahead."

Chance shook his head, taking a desperate step towards her. "No, it's not--"

Another attractive woman approached them. "I've been looking for you," she said to Stacy, looping her arm through hers.

"Julia, wait--" Stacy said sending Chance a quick look as if she wanted to say more.

Tameka rubbed his lips with her finger, making her possession of Chance clear. "Sorry, baby I got lipstick on you."

"Excuse us," Julia said with a cool glance then led Stacy away.

He spun around to Tameka. "What the hell was that?"

She blinked at him surprised. "What? I thought you'd be happy?"

"Happy?"

"You looked trapped. I was trying to save you."

Chance swore and hung his head.

"Wasn't she coming onto you pretty strong?"

"Never mind," Chance said watching Julia take Stacy far across the room. "Forget it."

~

"WHAT ARE YOU DOING?" Stacy asked, pulling away from Julia.

"Stopping you from making a fool of yourself. Do you know how many women have made a beehive towards him in the last hour?"

Stacy put her phone and stylus away with trembling fingers. She hadn't expected Chance to be so cold. At first her heart leapt when he stood and flashed his engaging smile and his beautiful eyes sparkled with amusement, that was until he recognized her. Then all the charm disappeared, like he'd flipped a switch. "He was alone when--"

"Well, he's not anymore."

Stacy turned and saw Chance surrounded by two other women in addition to Tameka. She sighed. "I just wanted to talk to him."

Julia lightly patted her on the back like a wise older sister. "You just suffered a moment of weakness. That's why I'm here to rescue you. He's moved on and so should you."

"Who is she?"

"Which one?"

Stacy jabbed her friend with her elbow, knowing Julia was being obtuse to prove her point. "You know which one. *His date.*"

"She's an actress. Don't look surprised. What did you expect? A teacher?"

"Chance isn't like that, if he likes her it's for other reasons than her looks."

"He may be interested in you for other reasons."

"What do you mean?"

"I just got word that Chance is interested in the part of Melvin."

Stacy laughed.

"I'm serious."

Stacy shook her head. "That's not going to happen. He's all wrong for it."

"I agree, but I heard from two key contacts who are really pressing his case, which I found surprising considering he works without a manager or agent."

"Hubris?" Stacy asked knowing that wasn't the case, but wanting to sound unbiased.

Julia sent Chance a considering look. "Or maybe he's just smarter than we think. Be careful Stacy he may have a hidden agenda."

$\sim$

HE COULDN'T FOCUS. Damn what had Stacy meant to say? What did Julia have to do with anything? Why did Tameka have to come at the wrong moment? Did she really miss him?

"You're a million miles away," Tameka said.

"Sorry." It was now or never. He had to get his questions answered. He pulled out his cell phone and sent

Stacy a text then looked up at Tameka. "I'll see you later, okay?"

"Where are you going?"

"I just need a few minutes to figure out something," he said then left the room. Minutes later he stood in the second floor stairwell wondering if Stacy got his text and whether she'd reply. After fifteen minutes he leaned against the wall defeated. She wasn't coming. He was about to leave when he heard the door below him open, then Stacy appeared on the landing.

"Do you know how many stairs there are in this place?" she said breathless, leaning against the railing.

She came. Chance raced down the stairs, pulled her into his arms and kissed her, sinking into the pleasure of the sweet feel of her lips. She didn't pull back or draw away. Instead she deepened the kiss, her tongue darting inside his mouth. He felt his body grow hard; her soft form pressed against him. His hands explored the hollows of her back. "God, it would be so easy to get you out of this dress," he whispered then covered her mouth again.

After one long, delicious moment, she broke away. "Julia, can't know about this," she said in a hurried, anxious tone.

"Julia?" Chance asked, not really caring. Stacy was the only woman who mattered to him.

"The producer of *Courting Danger*, you just met her. I know you want a part and--"

"You think I'm here because I want a job?"

"No, but she does and when you audition--"

Chance shook his head. "I'm not going to audition. If it's a choice between you and a role, there's no contest." He kissed her again.

Stacy pressed her hands against his chest. "Chance--"

He glanced down and grinned. "You've got the right idea."

She stifled a laugh at his overt invitation. "We should stop. Someone could see us."

He lifted her arm and kissed his way up to her shoulder. "So what?"

"What about your date?"

He kissed her neck. "She'll understand."

Stacy cupped his face in her hands, forcing him to look at her. "No one can know about us. At least not yet. Trust me. I'll call you when the auditions are over. Now I've got to go." She turned to leave.

Chance grabbed her wrist. "You can't just leave like that. I told you, I'm not interested in just being friends."

A sly, sexy grin spread across her face then she winked at him. "In case you haven't noticed." She kissed the tips of two fingers then placed them against his lips. "Neither am I."

$\approx$

STACY RETURNED to the ballroom feeling amazing. Beautiful, desirable and wanton. She still couldn't believe the text Chance had sent asking her to meet him.

"Where did you disappear too?" Julia asked her.

"The bathroom."

Julia narrowed her eyes. "Liar. You went to go see him. What did he say?"

Stacy couldn't help a grin. "Nothing."

"I bet you he said he's not interested in the role, just you." Julia looked at her friend with pity. "And if you believe that, get ready to get your heart smashed again."

CHAPTER FOURTEEN

DONALD MOTT WASN'T in a good mood. The past three weeks of auditions had not produced the actor he wanted. None of the over three hundred plus applicants had the quality he was looking for. He had a half hour before he had to return to Julia's office and hear another reading. He knew Julia and Stacy were already set on one known actor, impressed by his eight by ten glossy photo and impressive credentials. But Donald wanted something more. Someone fresh.

He stood in the hall chewing gum, instead of smoking like he used to. He was about to pull out another stick of gum when he spotted a striking figure leaning against the wall. There was something about the man's pose that drew him--intrigued him.

"Hey," he said.

The man straightened and Donald suppressed a smile, pleased by his height. He also looked curious, but approachable. "What?"

Donald handed him a script. "Come on."

The man glanced at the script then shook his head. "I'm not here to do a reading, I was just waiting for a friend."

"You're an actor, right?" He recognized the face, but couldn't place him, and at that moment wasn't particularly interested in who he was, he just needed a warm body. "Chase something?"

"Chance," he corrected without offense.

"Right. I want you to read for *Courting Danger*. You know about it?" He didn't give him an opportunity to reply. "Let's go."

~

STACY HID her surprise behind a coughing fit, when Chance entered the room. Julia offered her a cup of water and a smug look that said 'I told you so'. *What was he doing there?* It had only been two weeks since the fundraising gala. He said he wouldn't audition. Had he lied to her? Was Julia right and he was just using her? Had she been fooling herself? She'd believed him but now he was here. Stacy took a deep breath determined not to let any of her feelings show.

"I know he's not on the schedule," Donald said to Julia. He said something else but Stacy wasn't listening. She couldn't stop staring at Chance. Still trying to figure out why he was there. He couldn't possibly read for the role of Melvin. He was all wrong. What was Donald thinking? Chance seemed at ease, glancing over her as if she were a piece of furniture. She stiffened at the subtle slight, then realized he was being professional and she would be too. She watched him shake hands with Julia. She hadn't expected the casting of Marshall's character to be so difficult.

She'd expected the role of Shiree to be more of a struggle and it had been a little awkward since the character was based on herself, but she and the rest of the production team had felt that Melody Crane was perfect. Now they just needed the right piece to the puzzle. She wanted to scream that he was all wrong. They were wasting their time, but if Chance wanted the opportunity, she wouldn't stop him.

"We'll use the scene from the second act," Stacy said keeping her gaze on the script, she did the reading with all the actors. "Do you need some background?"

"I know enough," Chance said.

"Do you need a lead in?"

Chance shook his head. Distant, but obliging, reminding her of the kind doctor he played on TV or that man who'd smiled when he'd found her in the men's room. Then she watched him briefly close his eyes and take a deep breath. When he opened them, he stared at her with a piercing, razor sharp gaze that made the blood drain from her face, taking her into the story.

"Shiree," he said in a tone that gave her goose bumps. "Do you think it's easy for me out there? Do you know how much I work?"

"Yes, but that audition I got for you--"

"Was beneath me and you know it. Reputation is

everything. If I played a role like that, I'd be typecast for life."

"But you're more than one role," Stacy said reliving the moment she'd written about. Shocked that Chance had been able to embody Marshall's disdain with such perfection.

"I'm more than that role." He narrowed his eyes, a look of pleading despair entering them. "Do you even love me?"

Stacy wanted to turn away, but gazed back at him mesmerized. "Please don't do that. You know I do."

"Then why would you even think I'd do it? I'm a genius and I don't care how long it takes for the world to find out."

"But even a genius needs to eat."

"I thought you'd support me. What's a man to do when his own wife doesn't believe in him?"

"I'm not having this conversation." She turned.

He grabbed her wrist, but didn't force her to turn around. Instead he held her still and moved his lips close to her ear, his breath was warm but his words made her insides chill. "Don't walk away from me." He slowly walked around her and forced her to face him. This time the hurt and despair disappeared from his eyes, replaced with a cruel dominance. He deepened his tone. "When this conversation is finished, I'll let you know."

"Excellent!" Donald said. "We'll get back to you."

In an instant the chilly, arrogant expression left his face. Chance nodded. "Okay," he said then left without a goodbye.

Stacy dropped her gaze to the script, although she

wanted to run after him. She needed him. She needed his unexpected brilliance. He'd both horrified and mesmerized her. He took the role to the next level. The whole production would be more resonant with a performance like that. He could help her show the world that she didn't need Marshall to succeed. That she was her own woman and she could stand on her own. That she made quality work.

Donald looked satisfied with himself. "He's the one. Either he plays this role or I'm out," he said then his cell phone rang. He glanced at the number. "I have to take this," he said then turned and answered.

Julia swore. "You know what that means, right? If Chance is the only actor Donald will work with then we have to convince him to play the part. If not, it could sabotage the entire production. I already know of three actors who will walk if Donald isn't the director. Chance is one clever bastard."

"I don't think Chance orchestrated this," Stacy said, offended by Julia's distrust.

Julia sent Stacy a significant look. "Maybe not. Maybe he just happened to be here, and Donald just happened to choose him. Maybe. But I'll guarantee you this, the moment you offer him this role you'll be old news."

Stacy couldn't ignore the truth of her friend's words. He'd breezed in and out of the room as if they were strangers. Donald was right. He was perfect. He was on the cusp of a new level of stardom and was still young enough not to be tied down.

Stacy rode the elevator with a feeling of dejection

when her cell phone buzzed. She looked at it and her heart leaped when she saw a text from Chance.

Meet me. He said then gave her a location in Central Park.

Stacy bit her lip then sent him her reply.

CHAPTER FIFTEEN

THE SLIGHT BITE of early autumn chilled the air, but few leaves had changed their colors yet. Stacy watched a family of four walking carrying balloons and a group of joggers make their way past her. She glanced at her watch again, wondering if she'd gone to the right spot. Then she saw him running towards her carrying a small bouquet of flowers. He quickly kissed her. "Sorry, I'm late and I can't stay long, but I had to see you. Here," he said handing her the flowers.

"What are these for?" Stacy said taking the flowers and smelling them.

"I didn't plan on auditioning. I was--"

"It's okay. You were perfect."

"I don't want you to think I was lying to you." He led her over to a bench and they sat. He rested his arm behind her and let his hand graze her neck, his fingers cool and smooth against her skin. His expression grew serious. "Stacy--"

A young woman with corkscrew curls came up to him. "Excuse me?" When he looked up she clapped her hands together and grinned. "I knew it was you. You've got to tell me what happens next."

A slow smile spread on his face. "My lips are sealed, but you won't be disappointed," he said then winked.

The woman blushed then hurried away.

Chance turned to Stacy and just as quickly as he'd made the other woman blush, his intense brown gaze made Stacy feel as if she were the only woman in the world. "How are things with Houdini? I know of a great dog park."

"He's doing much better," Stacy said with a laugh. "I had to get rid of my last dog sitter and I now drop him off at a Doggie Day Care when I can't be at home. I know he'll love to see you."

Chance tucked a strand of her hair behind her ear, his knuckles brushing against her cheek in a tender caress. "Thanks for coming."

"You were brilliant at the reading," Stacy said not knowing what else to say. "How did you do that?"

He rested his arm behind her and shrugged. "I got into character. I enjoy it when I get to play someone complex and full of contradictions."

"You understand him well."

Chance lowered his head and licked his bottom lip, briefly reminding Stacy of someone, but then the memory faded. "I'd better, if I want him to come alive on screen."

Stacy suppressed a grin. He was interested in the

part, Donald would be happy. "Do you relate to him? Do you understand him?"

"Sure. But am I like him? No. He's full of insecurities that makes him push away the very woman he loves and the life he loves."

"He only loves himself."

"If that were true he wouldn't be so miserable. He lives with a mask on."

"And you don't?"

"No, what you see is what you get. Wearing a mask would be exhausting. But for a few hours I can be whoever you want me to be," he said with a devilish glint in his eye.

He was a true chameleon. He could seduce her with a casual glance, a simple touch or the tone of his voice, but was it real or just an act? She couldn't be sure. "So you're interested in playing the role?"

"I'm really not sure yet. Tell me about Julia."

Stacy pulled out her cell phone. "She's a fabulous producer and--"

Chance covered her hand. "I don't want her resume. I want to know why you warned me about her."

"She thinks I'm making a mistake seeing you. It has nothing to do with you personally," she said quickly, when she saw his expression darken. "She just doesn't trust me with actors, especially after my ex."

Chance paused. "Do you still want to see me?"

"Yes."

"Do you want me to take the role?"

"Yes."

"Then there's only one way you'll convince me."

Stacy leaned forward eager to hear him. She was so close to getting all that she wanted. *I'll do anything*, she wanted to say, but instead said, "What?"

"Remember who I am."

She sat back confused. "Remember who you are? I know who you are. You're Chance Jamison the actor on a popular TV show...why are you shaking your head?"

"That's who I am now. I want you to remember who I really am."

"Who you really are?"

"You're starting to sound like a parrot."

Stacy rubbed her forehead. "I'm sorry, but I don't understand."

"We met before. A long time ago. I want you to remember that."

"Why?"

"Because the moment you remember me, you'll remember the woman you used to be." He stood. "You have three days."

Stacy jumped up and grabbed his arm. "But that isn't fair. Maybe you're confusing me with somebody else."

"I'm not."

"At least give me a hint. How long ago? Was it at school? Where did we meet?" She lifted up his shirtsleeve.

Chance grinned. "Checking for tattoos? I don't have any and don't worry, we weren't that close. Even though I wanted to be." He winked. "There's your hint. Good luck."

"Wait," Stacy said before he could turn "Are you

saying you don't want to see me again? Was I cruel to you?"

"No, anything but. I just won't play Melvin until you remember. I want you to trust me. By remembering me, you'll know you can trust me." He turned and walked away. Stacy fell hard onto the bench.

She'd met him before? Who the hell was he? Why couldn't she remember? She would have definitely remembered someone like him. Why didn't she?

$\approx$

"He says I know him," she told Julia that night over the phone.

"Of course you know him."

"From before. He said we met before, but I don't remember." She paused. "He did seem familiar when I first saw him, but I can't place him. I must have seen him on TV before. I don't understand why it's so important."

"Make it important. You have to remember. Look up his background, look at old photos something will trigger a memory."

Stacy spent the next two days in total misery. She did an online search but only found superficial information about Chance. Where he'd been born, what his real name was before he changed it, but even that information didn't ignite any memories. She didn't see him in any of her photos and all her old diaries were filled with Marshall. She decided to go to a downtown bar to drown her sorrows. Stacy sat alone in a booth looking at the other patrons with envy, imagining them having better lives than she had. She'd failed even before she'd begun.

But she couldn't accept the option of failure. She wanted Chance in her film. Why couldn't she remember him? Had she really blocked out so much of her past that she'd forgotten a wonderful person like him? Stacy sighed and glanced up in time to see a portly white man coming from the direction of the men's room, zipping up his trousers. A beautiful black woman soon followed, adjusting her skirt. Stacy paused when she recognized her: Laurice. Their eyes met and Stacy called her over with a silent gesture of her hand. For a moment Stacy thought she'd ignore her, but Laurice got a drink then joined her at the table.

"Long time no see," Stacy said.

"Hmm."

She noticed the bruise on queen's jaw. "What's that?"

"A love tap," she said taking a sip of her drink. "What do you want?"

"I just wanted to say hi and tell you that the story you wrote for the last class was amazing. I never got a chance to tell you."

Laurice took another sip. "Hmm."

Stacy waited, half expecting queen to get up and leave, but when she didn't she decided to drop the pretense. "So what's up with the men's room?"

"It's my express special," she said with a smile. "Although that guy took a long time to get going," she said making a crude gesture with her hand.

"You're toying with going back inside."

Laurice shrugged, clearly unconcerned. "It's what I

do. I'm a free agent now. I don't have nobody telling me what to do."

"Don't you want more?"

Laurice sniffed and looked at Stacy as if she were a naive child. "We all want more, that doesn't mean we'll get it."

"True, but you're playing a dangerous game."

She shrugged.

"You're a beautiful woman."

"Doesn't matter when you're as dark as me."

Stacy pierced her with an icy glare. "Don't pull that skin color crap with me, that's not why you're here doing this. You've got too much pride and an inner will to make me believe that. I've seen women who hate themselves and you're not one of them."

Laurice smiled, flashing beautiful white teeth. "Man, I can't put nothing over on you."

"No, so give me another answer."

"I told you. I like being in business for myself."

"You could choose another business."

"With what? I don't got the connections or the education. And I'm too old for anyone to believe in me."

"You're never too old to turn your life around." Stacy finished her drink then carefully set it down. "We both ended up at the detention center due to bad choices. You've got so much more to offer the world and--"

"I don't need a lecture."

"How about a job?" Stacy said keeping her gaze on the glass in front of her.

"A job?"

Stacy took a deep breath then lifted her gaze. "I could use a housekeeper."

Laurice swore. Her lip curled with disgust. "You think I want to be cleaning toilets for minimum wage?"

"No, I don't. If you want to stay on the streets, that's your business, but I'd rather clean toilets than service men on them. You can have a different life. Instant gratification is a double-edged sword. One makes you believe today is all that matters and the other, that you'll always have tomorrow."

Laurice folded her arms, but still didn't leave. "Why are you being nice to me?" she finally asked.

Because you remind me of myself. That realization shocked Stacy because in truth they had little in common, but somehow she felt as if she'd found a soul sister. The Black Stockings Society had given her another chance and she wanted to offer that same opportunity to someone else. "Because I could use your help."

Laurice shook her head. "That's how bleeding hearts like you get into trouble. I could rob you blind."

"But you won't."

"Don't pretend that you know me."

"I'm not. If you want to end up in jail again, fine. I just think you're smarter than that."

"You got a big house?"

"No, but I do have a dog."

Laurice swore again.

"But you won't have to worry about where you sleep, what you eat or who calls you."

"I'm a businesswoman and you want to turn me into a cleaning woman?"

"That's one way of looking at it. Or you can take your business know-how and use it in another industry. Free-lancing and running your own business are two different things. As a freelancer you're at the whim of whoever hires you. When you run your own business the stakes change. Trust me, as a woman who knows. I can teach you a lot of things, but you have to be humble enough to start at the bottom." Stacy gripped her hand into a fist and met Laurice's steady gaze. "I was touched by an older cousin once, in a way I wish I could erase from my mind. The violating betrayal sliced through me like a machete and it took me years to build my self-esteem back." Stacy shook her head. "Sometimes I feel as if I'm still working on it. A female cousin of mine laughed at me when I got married. She was bold and free and slept with whichever man she wanted to, saying she'd never let one man have control over her body again like an Uncle did one summer with her."

Tears shined in Laurice's eyes, but she didn't move, her composure never wavered.

"But I didn't see her really in control of anything, just running from her pain. Or pretending that it wasn't there." Stacy scribbled down her contact information, not sure Laurice would want it. "Here's my address. You'd be my house manager. I have someone who comes once a week to clean, a dog sitter, when Houdini, that's my dog, isn't in daycare and I'm not home, and you'd supervise their schedules and have other tasks you'd be in charge of. Call when you're ready," she said then left, surprised she'd been able to keep her voice steady and her eyes dry. She hadn't spoken about what her cousin had done to anyone, but somehow she sensed it was a story Laurice needed to hear.

An hour later, Stacy sat on her couch, staring at the TV certain she'd lost her mind. What was she doing hiring Laurice when she didn't even know if the project would get off the ground? She should be focusing on who Chance Jamison was. Where she'd met him, and why her knowing him mattered so much. Instead she'd gotten sidetracked. She'd let her heart, instead of her head, rule her. Just as she'd hated the thought of Houdini not having a home, she hated the thought of Laurice living her life on her back or on her knees. It didn't matter, besides, Laurice probably wouldn't call.

The phone rang. Stacy absently picked it up. It was probably Julia wondering if she'd finally remembered Chance or not.

"I'm in the lobby," Laurice said. "They're giving me grief."

Stacy jumped up from the couch and vouched for Laurice with security so they'd allow her access to the elevators.

"That was fast," Stacy said opening the door.

Laurice looked around and gave a low whistle. "And I thought I made money."

Stacy sniffed. "And this is a downgrade."

"Someone could downgrade me to this any day." Laurice said touching the soft leather couch. "Where's my room?"

Stacy gave her a quick tour of her condo then let her settle in her private suite. After she fed Houdini, who took a while to settle down after meeting the new houseguest, Stacy went back to her research. She had one night left.

"What's all this?" Laurice asked looking at Stacy's papers and notes strewn on the dining room table.

"I'm meeting with an actor tomorrow, for lunch and have to convince him of something."

"Let me help you," Laurice said walking away. "Where's your bedroom again?" Laurice walked into Stacy's bedroom. She opened Stacy's closet and swore. "You're right. You know what you're doing. One day I want a closet like this."

Stacy only smiled, knowing that her wardrobe hadn't looked like that before the Black Stockings Society and Rania entered her life.

Laurice pulled out a dress. "You should wear this tomorrow."

"For lunch? Isn't that for a party?"

"You want him to do something, right?"

"Yes, but--"

"Men think with their eyes. If you want something, you have to tell him what it is. You know what you want him to think about? You. You want him so focused on you that he'll agree to whatever you say."

Stacy hated the thought of disappointing Chance. "I don't think he's that kind of man."

"Is he straight?"

"Yes."

"Are you his type?"

"Does it matter?"

Laurice grinned. "You like him."

"Yes," she said feeling defensive. "And I really need him for a role, that's all."

Laurice shook the dress. "Then let this dress persuade him while your mouth gets him to sign the deal."

~

"Do you know what your problem is?" Tyson asked Chance. They'd just finished a round of tennis at the private athletics' club they both belonged to.

Chance grinned. "Go on and tell me."

"You expect too much. I mean the role is yours. Why won't you just take it?"

He'd been asking himself that same question for the last two days. Why was he taking such a big gamble? What if she didn't remember, was he really willing to walk away? Did it really matter if she remembered him or not? He wanted her to remember the vibrant, bright Stacy she used to be when she didn't worry about people like Marshall or Julia. But who was he to tell her who she needed to be? Her lack of memory had bruised his ego and her past actions had hurt his pride. But was he really willing to sabotage an entire project? There were other people whose livelihood was tied up to this. And giving a desperate woman an ultimatum was not the kind of man he wanted to be. "I will."

"What?"

"Don't tell anyone yet until I've spoken to Stacy, but I'm taking the role."

"So she meets your terms."

No. "Yes."

"Whoa, you had everyone worried there for a minute. Did you see the doctor?"

"Yea, there's nothing to worry about." His doctor had given him another prescription that made him feel drowsy and he didn't plan on continuing. He was doing better practicing some mind and breathing exercises. He stopped a smile, wondering what Stacy would do if he had an attack with her. Maybe she'd remember then, considering he'd had his first attack with her and she'd stopped him from feeling as if he were dying. That was the key to everything. He wanted her to be impressed by what he'd become, instead she made him feel small. Forgettable. However, that wasn't her fault or his. It just was. She'd chosen to marry a man like Marshall. He'd made his choices too, some he regretted. Now, he'd start fresh with her and this time he'd make sure she never forgot him.

~

NEVER LET *an ex-hooker dress you for a business meeting.* Stacy tugged at the hem of her dress and shifted in her seat, resisting the urge to check her watch for the sixth time. She sat in the restaurant waiting for Chance feeling as conspicuous as red polka dots at a black and white tie event. She hadn't had so many men take notice of her in a long time and while it was flattering, it was also unnerving. She just needed one man to notice her black dress, stockings and heels. She needed him to forgive her for not remembering him, but Laurice had more confidence in Stacy's feminine wiles than she did. When she saw him coming towards her table she took a deep breath and prayed her plan would work.

Stacy crossed her legs and lazily ran her hand up and down her thigh. "Hi."

Chance's gaze dipped to her thigh, his expression giving nothing away before returning his look to her face. "Hi," he said taking a seat.

She uncrossed then crossed her legs again. "I'm really glad you're giving me this opportunity."

He covered her hand and his eyes bore into hers, a sexy grin touched the corner of his mouth. "You don't remember, do you?"

"What?" Stacy said her voice cracking with panic.

"You wouldn't have gone through all this trouble if you had."

"But--"

He shook his head, his smile tender. "Forget about trying to remember me. I don't care if you do or don't."

"The day hasn't ended yet."

"No, but I'm ready to put us both out of our misery," he said with a note of regret.

He was going to turn her down. She couldn't lose him, not a second time. She'd already lost him as a man she couldn't lose the actor as well. She seized his hand and held it between hers. "I'm sorry," she said louder than she planned, but not caring. She had to take the risk and let him know the truth. "I apologize for what I said about actors. I'm sorry about even mentioning just wanting to be friends. And I'm sorry that I don't remember you and know I should because you're an amazing actor and an amazing man." She shook her head at his look of surprise.

"But I'm not trying to flatter you just so you'll take this role, even though you're perfect for it," she said, surprised by her own sincerity. All of a sudden the role didn't matter as much as it had. As she held his hand, cradled in hers, she didn't just notice how large it was, the length of his fingers, but near his wrist she felt his pulse and realized how important he'd become to her. "This role will do wonders for you career."

Chance shook his head. "Stacy, don't."

"I don't care what Julia thinks or anyone else. I don't care if people think you're using me or that I'm making a mistake again." She hurried through her next words when she saw his jaw twitch. "Please take the role."

The buzz of his cell phone interrupted his reply. "Excuse me," he said checking the number. "Sorry, I have to take this."

"Go ahead."

He sighed then answered. He listened for a moment and his expression changed, replaced by a darker look. "Okay, I'll be right there." He disconnected then stood. "I've got to go."

Stacy looked up at him worried. "What's wrong?"

"I have to get a taxi."

"I've got my car. Where do you need to go?"

"Foster Elementary."

"What's going on?" Stacy asked leading him to where she had parked her car. Why would he need to go to an elementary school?

"There's a problem with my niece, Tiffany. She's locked herself in the girls' bathroom and won't come out."

CHAPTER SIXTEEN

"TIFFANY, IT'S ME UNCLE CHANCE," he said, as he poked his head around the corner of the girls' bathroom.

"Please go away."

Stacy looked at him. "How old is she?"

"Ten. She'll be eleven in June."

"Let me talk to her in private."

He hesitated, then nodded and left.

"Tiffany, hi, I'm Stacy Price. I'm a friend of your Uncle so you can trust me and tell me what's wrong?"

"Is Uncle Chance gone?"

"Yes."

"I don't want to upset him. I'm going to die."

"Why?"

"I'm bleeding to death."

"Tiffany, I don't think you're dying."

"I am. It's...it's coming from...you know...down there."

"Did your mother tell you anything about having a period?"

"A what?"

"In school, didn't you learn about becoming a woman in health class?"

"No, Mom wouldn't let me take that class."

Then she should have told you herself, Stacy thought wishing she didn't have to take on the task herself. "What's happening to you is perfectly normal. You're becoming a woman and every month a woman goes through a cycle."

"A cycle? What kind of cycle?"

Damn, how was it possible for a young girl, today, with so much information out there, and more openness, to still experience their first monthly flow in such an antiquated and scary way? But then, maybe her mother hadn't learned much either. Stacy spent the next fifteen minutes explaining the basics.

"I don't feel well."

"I know, we'll get you taken care of okay? I'll be right back."

"Don't tell Uncle," Tiffany said with a tremor in her voice.

"I won't." Stacy left the bathroom.

Chance raced up to her. "Is she going to be okay? Do I need to speak to her?"

"No, just give her a minute and she'll be fine."

"What's wrong?"

"Nothing. When she's ready, she'll tell you herself." Stacy held up her hand. "Don't ask any more questions, just trust me."

Stacy met with the school nurse, who helped take care of the crisis. After a few minutes, Tiffany came out of the toilet stall, tear faced. She was a pretty girl with light brown hair, big dark eyes and skin. On the drive home she remained quiet and tense no matter how much Stacy tried to make her smile.

"Is your Mom home?" Chance asked.

"I think so," Tiffany said in a tense voice.

"Then why didn't you--" Stacy let her word 'call' die on her lips when Chance sent her a curt look. But the question still lingered. If Tiffany's mother was home, why had the school called her Uncle? Stacy said nothing. When they reached her house, Tiffany quickly said, "Thank you," before jumping out of the car. Chance turned to Stacy and said, "Wait in the car" and left before she could argue. Stacy watched them with interest. They both seemed worried about something, but she couldn't guess what. They disappeared inside the house.

She had gotten a reprieve. He hadn't told her if he'd take the role, but the way he'd held her hand and said her name made her forget about him playing the role. Being with Chance made her only see a man. A wonderful man she wanted to get to know more. She still didn't remember him. She wished that looking at his niece would have given her an idea, but it didn't. Stacy looked around the clean cut neighborhood then glanced at her watch. They'd been inside at least ten minutes. She got out of the car and stood to stretch her legs then she saw the front door swing open and a cute, dark haired woman, wearing a shapeless brown dress that reminded Stacy of Idaho potatoes, came barreling down the stairs pointing at her, anger blazing in her eyes.

"You had no right!"

"I'm sorry?"

"You had no right telling my daughter things that should only be taught at home!"

Stacy stared at the woman openmouthed for a moment then shook her head. "What?"

"You told her about 'becoming a woman'."

Stacy felt her temper snap. "If you'd told her, I wouldn't have had to. She was terrified."

"I was going to have that talk in due time. She's fast and that's why it came sooner than I expected."

"You can't predict when the 'first time' will happen."

"I didn't get mine until I was nearly fifteen. These kids nowadays are just growing too fast."

Chance ran outside. "Maris!"

The woman ignored him and glared at Stacy. "Stay away from her."

"I was only trying to help," Stacy said trying her best to keep her tone civil. "I didn't tell her anything she shouldn't have known. I left plenty of space for you to fill in."

Chance took Maris's arm. "Come on back inside."

She yanked her arm away. "You told her about tampons."

"As an option," Stacy said.

"No ten year old should be shoving things inside herself that don't belong there. What if she makes it a habit and starts wanting to have other things put there?"

"I think you're taking this out of proportion."

Chance again tried to take the woman inside. She shoved him back. "You're as bad as she is." She spun back to Stacy. "You see how pretty she is? You think men aren't already thinking things. She's already a liability to me. I'm not having a girl that gets knocked up. Or maybe somebody will steal her and use her up."

"She's safe and I'm sure she's not even thinking about boys that way yet."

"Yes, she is. And now her innocence is gone." The woman's face crumbled to tears. "This is one of the worst days of my life." Her feet began to give way.

Chance grabbed her by the waist and lifted her up. "You need to rest."

"No!" She bit his arm so hard she drew blood. He loosened his grip and she lunged at Stacy, grabbing her arm in a vise-like grip. "You're seeing my brother, aren't you?"

"Let go of me," Stacy said in no mood to offer any explanation about her relationship with Chance.

Maris sneered, her nails biting into Stacy's arm. "Sure, you'll be sleeping with him soon, if you're not already. That's what women do these days. Especially women like you, dressed like that, ready to spread their legs for any--"

"That's enough," Chance said in a low voice, holding the back of his sister's neck in a way that forced her to release Stacy's arm. "Now you're going to calm down and go back inside and make sure your daughter is okay. Is that clear?" he said, releasing her.

Maris rubbed her neck and nodded then looked at Stacy and spat in her face.

Chance swore.

Maris laughed.

Stacy saw red. For a moment she wanted to take off her heel and whack Maris with it--hard. Then she remembered the punching bag at her anger management class, the women at the detention center and where her anger had gotten her before. She wouldn't strike back. No matter how unfair she felt Maris's treatment was, it wasn't worth the battle. Stacy took out some tissue from her bag and wiped her face, making sure to avoid Chance's gaze, then walked back to her car. She watched Chance take his sister's arm and this time she allowed him to lead her inside.

"She's filthy," Maris said loud enough for Stacy to hear.

"You think bikinis are filthy," he said in a tired tone.

"And they are. And Mom's expecting you home for Sunday." But that was all Stacy could hear before their voices faded inside. Stacy got in her car.

Chance emerged minutes later with his arm bandaged and in a dark mood. "Don't move," he said, sitting in the passenger seat and pulling out a swab from a small first aid kit he'd taken from the house. He dabbed at the scratch marks on her arm.

"It's--"

"Shut up and let me do this."

She did. When he'd finished, he sat back and stared out the window.

"Do you want me to drop you at a subway station?" Stacy asked not knowing what else to say.

He shook his head. "I'm sorry I didn't stop her. I didn't realize she'd gone outside until...until she got to you."

Stacy lightly touched his leg, feeling the tension in him. "I'm fine. Relax."

"My sister wasn't always like that. After her husband

left her she's put a tighter rein on Tiffany and it's getting worse." He glanced down at Stacy's hand. "I'm very angry right now."

Stacy stared at him stunned. He looked tense, mildly annoyed but not upset. "This is you angry?"

He nodded, his jaw twitched but his tone remained neutral. "Very."

"You look as calm as a choir boy."

"That's because I know how to fool people." His gaze pierced hers. "I know how to make people think I'm one way, when I'm really another." He shifted fully in his seat, resting his hand on the dashboard, making the space in the car feel smaller. "I'm good at that."

Both his tone and look made her believe him. And a shiver of awareness shimmered through her as she looked into the gaze of a man with many hidden depths. Depths she wanted to fall into. "I know. That's why you're perfect for the role--"

Chance drummed his fingers on the dashboard, but his gaze never wavered. "Don't play games with me, Stacy."

"I'm not," she stammered, suddenly unsure of how to read him.

"Don't tell me it doesn't matter if people think I'm using you."

"But it doesn't."

"Yes, it does." He fell silent for a moment. "Do you think I'm using you?"

"No."

"If I don't take this role will you still want to see me?"

"There's a lot at stake."

"What if I told you that I don't particularly like Julia and I've worked with directors less annoying than Donald? Whose side would you take? Mine or theirs?"

Stacy shook her head. "You don't understand, I need this project to work."

"I do understand, but what I'm asking you right now is am I just an actor or am I your man? If I'm just an actor then if I say no or yes determines whether I'll see you again. But if I'm your man that won't matter."

Stacy closed her eyes and rested her head back. "You're making this complicated."

"Actually, it's very simple. Which is it?"

Am I your man? What a question. What a choice. Did she really have to make one? But he was right. They couldn't have questions between them. Stacy groaned then rested her head on the steering wheel, resisting the urge to bang it. "Julia's going to kill me."

"What does that mean?"

Stacy turned to look at him. "That means you're my man first and an actor second. And Julia's going to think I'm an idiot and that I'm ruining my career again."

"Forget about Julia."

"She's the only friend who stood by my side. She's a good person. I don't know why you don't like her."

Chance drew her close. "I don't like anyone who makes you doubt yourself."

"She worries about me."

"Then we have something in common. Julia isn't the only producer around. I have my own company. Depending on the contract you signed, you have options."

Stacy sat back and frowned at him. "I know," she said

then reached over and smoothed down his eyebrow. "So how does it feel?"

"What?"

"Being my man?"

The beginnings of a smile tipped the corners of his mouth. "I like it. Let me show you how much." He pulled her close and covered her mouth with his. "Do you like being my woman?" He whispered against her lips.

"Uh huh," she said.

"That's good to know," he said then kissed her some more.

And Stacy let herself surrender into the deliciousness of the kiss until a thought entered her mind. She quickly drew away. "Stop."

"Why?"

"We can't make out like this in front of your sister's house. She already thinks I'm a--"

"I don't give a damn what she thinks." He sighed. "But you're right."

"What subway station do you need?"

He told her then looked at his watch and swore. "I have a meeting in three hours and it will probably run late."

"Rain check?" Stacy said, putting the car in gear.

"Will you still be up by nine?"

"Yes."

"Good." He grinned, making her heart melt. "And don't change."

CHAPTER SEVENTEEN

DON'T CHANGE. But of course that was the first thing Stacy did when she got home. She jumped into the shower, wanting to be as clean and fresh as possible before he arrived, but she didn't make it to the bathroom before having to field Laurice's questions first.

"So did it work?" she demanded meeting Stacy at the front door.

Stacy walked past her. "I'm not sure yet."

"What do you mean you're not sure?" Laurice followed close behind.

He hadn't said he'd take the role, but he did want to be with her. "He's coming over tonight. I have to get ready."

An hour later Stacy was wearing a new perfume, the same dress and a new set of nerves.

"What do you want me to do?" Laurice asked, watching Stacy plump up several pillows in the living room.

"Nothing. Just make yourself scarce."

Laurice grinned. "Oh, it's going to be that kind of night?"

"I hope so."

The door bell rang.

Stacy looked at the clock. "He's early."

"Do you want me to hide?"

"No," Stacy said going to the door. "I'll introduce you and then--"

Laurice smiled. "I know."

Stacy took a deep breath then opened the door. "This is a surprise. I thought you had a meeting."

"I cancelled," he said, then covered her mouth with his.

Stacy drew away, breathless. "Come inside. I have to introduce you to..." her words trailed off when she realized no one else was in the room, not Laurice, not even Houdini.

"Who?" he asked in a husky tone.

"Um...nobody," Stacy said, her heart beating madly in her chest, acutely aware of him.

"So, where's the little fella?" Chance asked. "I thought I'd see him."

"Oh, Houdini's with my housekeeper."

Chance pulled her into his arms and closed the door with his foot. He kissed her then dropped his mouth to her neck and inhaled her scent. "Hmm...you smell good."

"I had a shower," she said then inwardly groaned at making such a banal statement.

Chance didn't seem to care. "I wish I'd been there," he said, his breath hot against her skin. Then in two smooth movements, he unzipped her dress and it fell to the ground.

Stacy gasped and covered her chest and front. She wasn't wearing anything underneath--except for a pair of sheer black stockings. Stacy stared at him stunned. "I thought you wanted me to wear this dress."

"Yes," Chance said letting his heated gaze slide seductively downward. "Just so that I could do what I just did. I've been imagining how all day. But I never imagined this."

"No," Stacy said frantically reaching for the dress, never expecting her surprise to be revealed in the foyer.

He tossed the dress out of reach. "Don't be shy. Let me see you."

"I didn't expect to walk around naked," Stacy said feeling both embarrassed and aroused by his smoldering glare.

"Relax," he said unbuttoning his shirt. "You won't be the only one." He tossed his shirt on the ground then he held out his arms and glanced down at his jeans. "You can do the rest."

Stacy didn't move, still standing like Eve caught without her fig leafs. "Close your eyes."

"Why?"

"Just do it."

Chance slowly shook his head as if he thought she were a little dense then did.

Stacy hooked the front of his jeans. "Now follow me," she said, tugging him towards her bedroom. "And---" she let out a startled gasp when he scooped her up in his arms.

"Lead the way, but this is faster," he said carrying her down the hall.

"Chance--"

"I'll take you right now if you don't start giving me directions."

"Go around the corner and down the hall. No, not this one," she said quickly when he stopped at the first door--Laurice's suite. She pointed to the one further down the corridor. "That one."

Chance lifted a brow. "Hmmm, a locked room. Are you keeping secrets?"

"Do you really care about my secrets right now?"

Chance pretended to think for a moment then carried her into her bedroom, laid her on the bed and removed the rest of his clothes.

"I thought you were going to let me do that."

"You lost your chance," he said kissing her again, his body covering hers.

"But I thought my Chance was right here," she said sliding her hand down his thigh.

He groaned. "I should have seen that coming."

She glanced down. "I can definitely see you coming."

"Are you always this corny in bed?"

"Yes," Stacy giggled. "I'm corny when I'm horny."

Chance laughed. "Then I'd better get you to stop talking." And he did, but not in a way she'd expected him to. He slipped off her stockings then teased her center with his tongue sending her soaring on a wave of desire that made her whole body tremble in ecstasy. Then she felt his warm, wet lips on her breasts, her chest, her neck, stirring her emotions into a fevered frenzy. She hadn't expected this--his gentle exploration. He touched her as if he worshiped her, as if she meant something to him. Marshall had been a selfish lover, leaving Stacy not only feeling exhausted but worn.

Chance made her feel immortal. Like a goddess and when he entered her she felt revered instead of possessed. Honored instead of disgraced. In his arms she felt beautiful, wondrous, amazing. She loved him, the thought frightened her a little, but her body told her not to care. And that night she let her heart take the lead, allowing herself to feel once again when she'd felt numb for so long. She let her senses become acute to the sensation of the hair on his legs brushing hers, the feel of his heartbeat against her chest, his rich brown skin as smooth as an untouched lake.

And like a lake, she wanted to dive into him, arching her body into his, tightening around him until he moaned. She let her body tell him what words couldn't and he seemed to understand her completely, as if he'd been waiting for this moment a lot longer than a day. But she didn't want to ask any questions.

Stacy lay in his arms, both her body and mind alive.

"Does this mean you'll take the role?"

She felt, rather than heard, him laugh. "Yes," he said then promptly fell asleep.

~

"THE MAN IS A GENIUS. A BARRACUDA," Julia said with feeling. They sat in a salon where Julia had decided to treat them to a pedicure. "You would not believe all that he demanded! He and his lawyer were vicious. No wonder he can play Melvin so well."

"What do you mean?" Stacy asked, not liking her friend's comparison of Chance to her ex.

"That it's not just his looks that have gotten him this far. He's smart. I've never met such a business savvy actor. He wants to be co-producer and I won't bore you with the rest. He knew he had the upper hand. He sliced through every bluff we put up."

"You can afford it."

"That's not the point. Who is he really?"

"He's not hiding anything. He told you what he wanted."

"He's a lot smarter than Marshall."

"That's because he isn't him."

"Love makes you blind, Stacy."

"I'm not in love with him," she lied.

"That's good, because I guarantee you, he has secrets and I think he has heartbreaker written all over him."

CHAPTER EIGHTEEN

NOBODY SAID no to Althea Paige. Chance had hoped to convince his mother he couldn't make the quarterly family dinner, but he'd failed. Chance sat at his mother's dinner table staring at the sight of salted fish, washed and chopped and stewed along with spinach, okra, coconut milk, and several seasonings in a chicken stock with, of course, dumplings. The scent of pumpkin fritters filled the air.

But despite the fine meal and how much he loved his family, Chance would have preferred spending time with Stacy. To his surprise she'd sensed his reluctance to go when they'd taken Houdini to the dog park and he watched the puppy make friends and chase falling leaves.

"What's wrong?" Stacy asked nudging him with her elbow.

He turned to her surprised. "What?"

"I hope you don't still feel awkward about the incident I had with your sister."

"I don't."

"Then why aren't you happy?" She took his hand and squeezed it. "I know I'll miss you this Sunday, but we'll have other times together."

"My sister is just the tip of the iceberg when it comes to crazy." He paused. "Wait, I shouldn't have said that. It came out all wrong."

"Everybody has family drama. I'm not going to judge you for it."

He knew she wouldn't, but that's what made it harder. It was getting harder and harder for him to be as understanding as he once had been. Harder and harder for him to ignore the cracks in the family bedrock he was starting to see. Harder to ignore that his grandmother needed care that his mother couldn't give and that his sister's roller coaster emotions needed to be addressed and then there was his mother. Althea was a woman with a beauty as cold as a glacier, and a temper as hot as the Sahara. A woman he loved who had the ability to hurt him like no one else could. She couldn't let a family dinner pass without reminding him that he was in a Peter Pan profession while his younger brother, Leon, did *real* work. His mother didn't disappoint him that Sunday either. Only five minutes into the meal she said, "I was watching one of your hospital scenes and heard you sounding off a lot of scientific terms. Do you even know what thrombosis is?"

"Mom, leave him alone," Leon said sending Chance a look.

"I just thought he sounded impressive for a boy who barely graduated high school."

"Look," Chance said tired of the same topic. "Everyone knows it's make believe. Leon's the real hero, not me."

"Too bad more people don't think that way, Terrell," she said.

"Chance," he corrected.

"I still don't know why you chose that name."

Maris spoke up. "Go on and tell them. Tell them what you did."

Chance sighed. "I didn't do anything."

"He let one of his hussies tell Tiffany about the birds and the bees."

Chance gripped his fork and kept his voice low. "This is not the time or the place."

"What is she on about?" his mother asked.

"Tiffany got her period," Maris said.

The young girl looked around the table horrified. "Mom!"

"There's nothing to be embarrassed about," Althea said. "Men know about periods too. They get really upset when women miss them." She said sending her other son a look.

Leon held up his hands. "I told you it was a false alarm."

She waved her fork at him. "Wrap the little snake and you won't have to worry about any kind of alarms false or otherwise."

Maris waved her fork. "You shouldn't be having this conversation with Tiffany here."

"You're the one who brought up the subject," her

mother shot back. "The girl's so ignorant she probably doesn't even know where puppies come from."

"The pound," Tiffany said. "And puppy mills."

They all laughed.

She frowned. "What's so funny?"

Althea looked at her daughter. "That's the next talk you need to have with her or I will."

"So what's the hussy's name?" his grandmother asked.

Chance shook his head. "She's not a hussy, she's a screenwriter."

"What? She can't be both?" His mother said with a grin.

He knew she was just toying with him, but Stacy was too important a topic to joke about. "If you don't want me to come around anymore, just say so."

"I'm sorry, I was just having a little fun. I'm proud of both my boys," she said the words with a smile, although no one believed them.

An hour later, Chance sat on the back porch of his mother's New Jersey home with his brother.

"Don't let Mom get to you," Leon said. "She was just teasing about--"

"That topic's off limits."

"So when will we meet her?"

Chance leaned back and didn't reply.

Leon sipped his beer and wisely changed the subject. "Have you made up your mind yet?"

Chance rubbed the back of his neck, trying to ease the tension there. He still wasn't sure what to do with Tiffany and Maris. "I was just talking."

"So, what are you going to do now? Are you really

thinking of taking Tiffany away and breaking our sister's heart?"

"That's not what I said."

"But that's what you plan to do," Leon said.

"I care about both of them and I have a lot on my plate right now, but--"

"Oh, that's right because you're working on a film. Is that more important than keeping your family together?"

"She's getting worse. Can't you see that? She's calling Tiffany horrible names."

"She's just more conservative than we are," Leon said with a shrug.

"It's not that. I don't mind her believing in what she does. But Tiffany is scared and she's asked to live with me."

"And you think you'll do better? She'll never let that happen. She's convinced you live in Sodom and Gomorrah. Besides, with your schedule, you hardly have time for yourself."

"I'll make time and I'll make sure she's taken care of."

"You have nothing. You can't win."

Chance didn't like the thought of breaking up their family, but his sister worried him. "She's started drinking again. I found some bottles in the house."

"Not like before."

"But--"

"You trying to be a *real* doctor now?" Leon said with a sneer. "You don't think my diagnosis is sufficient enough?"

Chance sighed, remembering a time when he and his brother didn't argue as much, they'd been more of a team. But now they were always at odds. He remembered the pride he'd felt when his brother graduated from medical school, the picture he'd taken of him as a resident. He remembered when his brother had gotten his first luxury car and opened his practice. They'd both overcome a lot. Leon was one of the few people he could trust. "It's not that." He shook his head. "What do you want from me?"

"I want you to leave things alone. If you really love us, you'll forget what Tiffany said. She's just a kid. She doesn't know what she really wants." He rested a hand on Chance's shoulder. "Trust me, if something were really wrong Mom would do something about it."

"Mom's getting old and so is Gran. It's our job to look out for them."

Leon looked at him, his voice like ice. "I'll say this one last time. Leave it alone. Or you won't only break up this family but lose everything you've worked for. Do you really want your adoring fans to know who you really are?"

CHAPTER NINETEEN

SHE TRIED her best not to hate him. An elegant crystal chandelier hung over a grand marble foyer, but Stacy didn't see anything else on the set but Chance and Melody bringing her script to life. She watched Chance embody the character of Melvin. Somehow he knew what he had to project for this scene and he did it with brilliance. Melvin was a manipulator and a destroyer, but also hungry for attention, using his magnetic sex appeal to get what he wanted. Even though she'd written the scene, Chance had given it an added depth. She hadn't known that Melvin wanted Shiree to know that he didn't need her, although inside he knew he'd be lost without her. He resented his dependency on her. Chance had found a way to depict all that on the screen, to make the audience see his dual role. To see that he wasn't just a jerk and hate him, but to feel sorry for him.

That was what Marshall had done best. That was why he always won and seeing that reality played out

before her made Stacy's insides shrivel. She remembered
how the scene mirrored one of her own. The time when
they'd just moved into the grand house he'd always
wanted. She had dreaded this scene and watching it had
been worse. The studio was a perfect replica of what her
living room had looked like. She'd returned home from
having a great lunch with Julia, after an awards cere-
mony, only to find Marshall in a lip lock with another
woman.

She stood frozen, wondering why she was always the
villain. He'd lied to her so many times, she could no
longer tell the lies from the truth. Chance played him so
well--too well. She could see why the judge had made her
pay him alimony. She'd written him as the antagonist, but
Chance showed him as an anti-hero. The woman who
played Shiree held her own against him, but she could
also see clearly their need for each other. How they fed
each other's weakness and desires.

"What are you doing?" Shiree said standing in the
doorway. Aptly depicting the shock Stacy had felt.

"I'm just helping her with a role," he said, his female
companion disappearing into the corner of the room.

"Am I supposed to believe that?"

Melvin threw the script at her. "I wish I knew I'd
married such a damn prude."

Shiree lifted up the script and saw the screen
described as what she'd seen.

"That wasn't just a kiss."

"When will you learn to trust me?"

"I do, but--"

"Then show it." He stood and moved closer to her and

lightly touched a strand of hair. "You're the only woman who's ever understood me," he said like a dejected Apollo.

"I'm sorry," she said, her voice filled with guilt. She wrapped her arms around him.

Melvin hugged her, but behind her back his mouth spread into a self-satisfied smile. Stacy hadn't written that. Chance had embodied the character so much, the action was improvised, but it worked.

"Cut! Brilliant. I'm going to do a close up of that expression, it adds an extra dimension."

"Is it just me or is it hot?" Chance said.

Melody teased. "You are too good. One moment I want to slap you and the next I want to rip your clothes off."

He lifted a brow. "As long as you're gentle."

"If I wasn't married..." She fanned herself. "My husband's going to be a happy man tonight."

He laughed.

No, she didn't want to hate him, but at that moment she did. Stacy turned to leave.

"Stacy!" Chance said coming up to her. "Meet me in ten," he said then kissed her cheek and disappeared.

She just wanted to be away from him right now, but he looked so pleased with himself and he had done a great job, she couldn't abandon him. Ten minutes later, Stacy walked up to him in his dressing room and saw that he'd washed his makeup off. He looked like Chance again.

"I just--"

He put a finger to his lips, sat down and pulled her onto his lap.

"What are you--?"

He put his finger to his lips again. Then gently pressed her head down onto his shoulder.

She rested her head, not sure what he was up to. Then felt her tension release as she let the memory of the scene dissipate. She lifted her head and looked at him. His eyes half closed.

'Can I talk now?' she mouthed.

He smiled and shook his head. Then pressed her head down and held her close. She sighed with frustration. Before she could respond he said, "You look tired."

It surprised Stacy how comforting it felt to be in his arms, to feel the deep vibration of his voice, to feel safe with him. She felt the building of tears. She felt humiliated that she'd been so used. But he made her forget Marshall. This moment had never happened between them. He never cared about her feelings, what kind of day she'd had. Everything had always been about him.

"I don't know how you do it," Stacy said.

"What?"

"Switch so quickly between roles."

He shrugged. "I like being myself more than anyone else. Especially someone like Melvin. He's exhausting."

"Exhausting?"

"He wears so many masks and feeds off of people."

Stacy lifted her head and looked around as if searching for something. "Where is it?"

"What?"

"Your ego? I can't seem to find it."

Chance laughed. "Trust me, it's there."

"But aren't you waiting for me to tell you how great you were?"

"No."

"But didn't you get into acting to hear the sound of applause, to be the center of attention, to receive praise?"

"Those are all nice and I'm not going to say I don't enjoy them, but what I love most about acting are the stories I get to tell. I'm part of a unit and my job is to disappear into someone else so that you don't see me. I want to make you feel. When I was young, I loved how movies made me feel and I wanted to do that for others. Seeing the look on your face was enough for me. But now that it's over, I don't want you to think of Melvin or Marshall. I want you to think of me. Is that enough of an ego for you?"

"You're very grounded for an actor."

He shrugged. "I don't have the luxury or interest to get into the traps of the artistic temperament associated with my field. You're a writer, you've seen it. The depression, the drugs, the sex. It has its place, but I like to keep the drama at a distance. Leading a normal life helps me fuel my work."

It made sense. Maybe because Marshall had lived a life filled with drama he had nothing to give. He had such changeable moods.

She playfully squeezed his chin. "You look tired too."

He smiled. "But I'm happy." He lifted her up and stood, then set her back down on the seat and started to change. "What do you want for lunch? My treat," he said before she could argue.

"Anything."

"I think I can handle that."

"Oh, and tonight let's watch a movie. A good horror film."

Chance shook his head. "Sorry, I don't do horror movies. I hate being scared."

Stacy looked at him for a moment, wondering if he were joking. "Seriously?"

"Yes, I grew up with a mean SOB of a stepfather who loved violence and terrified me most days. I know what fear's really like. I used to make it my job to stop my brother and sister from crying." He grinned, looking a little sheepish as if he'd revealed too much. "I started acting early."

"I'm sorry."

"It's okay. It's just a sore spot for me. Growing up I loved action, adventure and comedy. They let me escape."

Stacy shivered, not fooled by his casual tone, the pain of his childhood briefly dimming the light in his eyes. Her own upbringing had been relatively drama-free, except for the various troubles her brother got into, but her parents always bailed him out. Chance's revelation helped get her warring emotions back in order. He wasn't Marshall. She was safe with him. "Okay, how about a comedy?"

He looked a little sheepish. "I'd wanted to see the recent film by Heisman."

Stacy stared at him stunned. Heisman wasn't known for blockbusters, but experimental, independent films. "You're a fan?"

"I've watched every film he's ever made. The man is amazing."

Her mouth curved into a teasing smile. "Sounds like someone has a serious guy crush."

Chance held up his hands. "Guilty. I watched my first Heisman movie at twelve. A sci-fi thriller. I enjoy acting, but eventually I picture myself behind the camera too."

"You've already done some short films through your company."

"But one day I want to do something bigger."

"Okay, we'll see a Heisman film."

Chance lowered his head, licked his lip and pumped his fist. "Yes," he said like a happy little kid who'd just gotten his favorite ice cream flavor.

Again, something about his action reminded her of someone, but then quickly vanished. She shook herself. Why couldn't she remember who?

Chance held out his jacket. "If you're chilly, put this on."

She wasn't cold, but liked the thought of wearing his jacket. Stacy put her hands in the pockets. She paused when she felt some soft material. "I didn't know you carried handkerchiefs."

"I don't," he said.

And he was right, because what she pulled out of his pocket was a pair of ladies' panties.

CHAPTER TWENTY

Stacy looked at them for a long moment then said, "What are these. No wait, better yet whose are they?"

Chance shook his head stunned. "I don't know."

"Don't lie to me."

"I'm not. I don't know who they belong to. I don't even know how they got there."

She wanted to believe him, but she'd let herself believe so many lies and half-truths in the past. Had this all been too good to be true? She slowly took off his jacket. "I need to go."

Chance blocked her path and grabbed her arms. "Stacy, please. I wouldn't. Please believe me."

She blinked back tears. She didn't even have her anger to protect her anymore. "I just need some time to think. Okay?"

He released her.

"I TOLD YOU SO, didn't I?" Julia said. She and Stacy sat in Julia's study eating a bowl of popcorn and looking at the TV. "Actors cannot be trusted. You've been trying so hard to look good and you've wasted it all on him."

"I didn't come over for you to tear him down," Stacy said, regretting her rash decision to tell her friend. "I just wanted to talk and figure out what to do next. He said they weren't his and he looked really shocked."

"A man always looks shocked when he gets caught."

Stacy fell silent knowing that was the reason she'd come to Julia. Her friend said out loud what she was thinking. Had she been deceived? Was she being used again? Being with Chance felt like a dream, maybe this was the reality. Then why did she believe him?

"Actors lie for a living. It's only been a few months. You don't know him that well."

"He says I do."

"And you believe him? You can't even remember him. Stacy, you know I love you so listen to me. This is a sign." Julia glanced at the TV then grabbed for the remote and quickly changed the channel.

"What did you do that for?" Stacy asked.

"No reason," Julia said avoiding her glance.

"Go back."

"No."

"Was it Chance?"

"No."

"Then let me see."

Julia sighed then switched back.

Stacy saw Marshall talking to a late night talk show host--handsome and charming as always.

"You don't want to watch this," Julia said.

"Yes, I do." She didn't, but couldn't seem to pull herself away.

"So what do you think about this new movie about your marriage?" the host asked Marshall.

"My ex is still using me for her material," he sat back looking self-satisfied. "I can't complain."

Stacy blocked out the rest of his words and just watched his mouth move. He was still winning, still portraying himself to the world as her Muse. Was she just a stepping stone to Chance? No, she'd seen him with his niece and his sister and he'd helped her with Houdini. He wasn't Marshall. Stacy finished her drink then set her glass down with a thud. "I believe him."

"What?"

"I believe the panties aren't his."

"Of course they're not his. They belong to some woman he's sleeping with."

Stacy shook her head. "No, he said he wouldn't and I believe him."

"You're fooling yourself. I think you don't want to believe you've made another mistake, so you're creating a story for him. This is the first time I really feel sorry for you and I can't take it. If you take him back, I can't be your friend anymore."

Stacy stared at her friend shocked. "You don't mean that."

"Yes, I do. I can't sit back and watch you go down the same road you did before. You're deluding yourself. You've fallen for an actor who just *happens* to need a role, who just *happens* to have his own company, who just *happens* to carry panties in his pockets."

"I know it seems strange, but I've changed. Can't you see that? Not just my clothes and hair, but inside." She tapped her chest. "I'm not as blind and naive as I used to be. Marshall was selfish, Chance isn't. He was there for me when I needed him."

"Conveniently so, don't you think? You were very vulnerable. You didn't see the man I negotiated with and the cold calculating gaze I met across the table. That kind doctor he plays on TV is definitely an act."

"Because that's what he does."

"Exactly," Julia said in a grim tone. "But how do you know when he isn't acting?"

～

CHANCE PACED TYSON'S OFFICE, feeling a major headache grip him.

"They have to be Tameka's," Tyson said.

"They're not. I asked her."

"Who else have you been seeing?"

"Nobody," Chance snapped. "I told you."

"Fine, let's retrace your steps."

"I've done it a thousand times and I can't think of anyone."

Tyson fell silent then snapped his fingers. "Maybe it was a fan."

Chance shook his head. "Usually they attach a note to let me know who they are."

Tyson sat up in his chair with interest. "You've had women slip you their panties before?"

Chance shot him a glance. "Try to stay on topic."

"I've never had a woman give me her panties. How does she let you know? Do you feel it when she--" He stopped when Chance leaned on his desk and glared at him. He waved his hands. "Never mind. So you're sure it's not a fan? Right, it's not a fan," he quickly said, when Chance rested his hands on his hips and sent him another dark look. He cleared his throat, knowing his friend was dangerous when he was in this mood. "Do you think it was prank?"

"I asked. Nobody will admit to anything. My life's not that exciting. I went to work and I visited Tiffany..." He paused when he saw Tyson's eyes widen. "No, it can't be."

"Your sister has a lot to worry about if it is."

"It's not hers."

"You've got to make sure."

Chance rubbed his forehead. "It doesn't make sense."

"Do you want to see Stacy again?"

"How am I supposed to find out?"

"Just ask her."

Chance threw up his hands. "You expect me to ask my niece if she put panties in my jacket pocket?"

"Treat it like a joke. You know how to do this. Call her. Think of Stacy."

He couldn't stop thinking about her. He could under-stand her sense of betrayal. He remembered seeing her face on the set that day. He'd brought the actress, Melody, to tears but when he looked at Stacy, he saw the true impact of his performance. Her face was pale--he could sense the strength she wrapped around herself to keep her face neutral, her emotions in check. But he could see them anyway. At that moment he'd wanted to go up to her and hold her, but the director called him so they could do some close up shots. He put on his role again, although he'd wanted to share a look with her, a wink to let her know that it was all make believe, that this was only a replica of her past, but that her future with him would be different. She'd left before he'd gotten the chance and now they had had this awful misunderstanding.

He dialed his sister's number, for the first time wishing she allowed Tiffany to have her own cell phone. "Maris," he said when she answered. "I need to talk to Tiffany."

"Fine."

Moments later Tiffany came on the line. "Hi Uncle."

"Hi." He paused. "Maris, get off the phone." He heard a sigh and then a click. "Tiffany--"

"You found it?"

"What was in my jacket?"

"Yes. A friend at school got some and gave me one. She said it's what women wear, but then Mom came into my bedroom, I didn't want her to see them, so I stuffed them into your pocket when you came to pick me up. I didn't know how to tell you."

He sighed. "I wish you had."

"They're pretty, but they don't fit anyway."

"Don't accept anymore gifts from your friend, okay?"

"Are you mad?"

"No," Chance said wondering how he was going to get Stacy to believe him.

~

IF YOU TAKE HIM BACK, *I won't be your friend anymore.* Julia's words seared in her mind. How could she risk a long term friendship for what could be a short term affair?

"What happened to you?" Laurice said when she returned from grocery shopping and found Stacy sitting on the couch, staring at the wall, absently stroking Houdini.

"I have to break up with Chance."

"You *have* to?"

"Yes, I found panties in his pocket and he couldn't explain how they got there. Julia's convinced he's cheating on me."

Laurice sat down beside her. "What do you think?"

Stacy shook her head and continued to stare at the wall. "I don't know anymore, but I'll lose Julia if..." She let her words fall away.

"If what?"

"If I make the same mistake again."

"Then she ain't your friend."

Stacy turned to her. "What?"

"Hell, you know how many mistakes I've made, but my girl Rockett's always got my back and I have hers. No matter what. You sure she's not jealous?"

Stacy laughed. "Jealous of what? You haven't met her

yet, but you've seen her picture. She's gorgeous, successful, has a loving husband and family."

"You're right. I haven't met Julia, but I have met Chance."

Stacy still remembered their first meeting. Unlike her, he'd gotten on with Laurice from the first moment.

"How come she never stops by here?" Laurice asked.

"She's busy."

"I may be wrong, but I don't think Chance is stepping out on you. Anyone who sees Chance with you knows how he feels."

Stacy wanted to believe her, but knew that Laurice had her own reasons for wanting Chance to stay around. One afternoon, Laurice had overheard Chance reading Stacy a script he was considering buying for his company and she started laughing.

"What's so funny?" he asked.

"It's nothing, except no girl would talk to her pimp like that."

Chance looked at her for a moment and Stacy held her breath hoping he wouldn't insult her either by asking her how she'd know or ignoring her.

"How would you write it?" he finally asked.

Laurice told him and then he offered to pay her as a consultant. But before she could reply Stacy said, "Send me the contract and she'll let you know." She turned to Laurice. "You know the streets, I know contracts, trust me."

And she did, getting enough work and even two small roles. Stacy knew she'd be looking for a new housekeeper soon. For a moment she looked at Laurice as a woman.

Could the panties be hers? Like Kelly, could she be doing something behind her back? Was there no one she could trust?

Laurice sat back and narrowed her eyes in disgust. "Go on and ask me."

"What?"

"You think I'm doing your man."

"Are you?"

"No."

Stacy nodded relieved. "Okay."

Laurice sat up and blinked. "You believe me?"

"Yes, now call me stupid or a deluded idiot for trusting you. Go ahead and lie to my face and sleep with my man behind my back and make a fool out of me."

"I'd never do that to you. And a true friend would never think you're a fool."

Her home phone rang.

"That's probably him," Laurice said when Stacy didn't move. "You should talk to him."

"Answer it for me."

Laurice jumped up and answered the phone. "Okay, come up." She hung up then turned to Stacy. "He's down-stairs and will be here soon." Laurice grabbed Houdini's collar and made herself scarce.

She didn't know how she should face him. Should she be cool and distant? Neutral? Hopeful? Worried? Angry? Hurt? By the time he reached the door she was a jumble of nerves. But the look on his face subdued them all. She didn't see Marshall's charm or Chance's smile. She saw a man who looked vulnerable. And with that one look she knew their relationship mattered to him. That she mattered. She didn't see lust in his gaze or desire or even a plea--only complete surrender.

He stepped inside and closed the door behind him. "They're Tiffany's."

"What?"

"I know it's hard to believe," he rushed on. "But I spoke to her and she told me--"

"I believe you," she said, her heart breaking a little, knowing that her words meant she'd lost a friend. She hugged him, pressing her cheek against his chest. She closed her eyes against her tears, making a silent plea. *Please don't be lying to me. Please be the man I think you are.*

Chance gathered her close and she sunk into the warmth of his embrace. "You never have to worry about me. I promise you."

"I know," Stacy said trembling a little as she remembered Julia's words: He's an actor, how do you know when he's not? But this was real, Stacy thought. I know it is.

Chance pulled away and gazed down at her. "What's wrong?"

"Why?"

"You're shaking."

"I'm just so happy," she said, not ready to tell him about Julia's threat.

"Oh," he said feigning disappointment. "I thought you were cold and needed me to warm you up."

Stacy grinned. "Now that you mention it." She hugged herself and shivered. "I am a little chilly."

He let his hands slide a sensual path down her arms. "Where?"

"All over."

His heated gaze lazily surveyed the length of her. "Do you want to warm up fast or slow?"

She led him to the bedroom with a smile. "Slow."

~

AUTUMN TURNED to winter settling over the city with white clouds and thick snow, they went to plays, movies, attended the Macy's Thanksgivings Day parade and, over the holidays, Stacy introduced Chance to her family. Her brother tried to convince Chance to invest in a project, but Chance wisely ignored him. However, when Stacy offered to meet his family, Chance came up with reasons why she couldn't. At least not yet. He wrapped up his work on the film, *Courting Danger*, and Stacy sold a play to a theatre company, excited to be involved with the stage again. In the New Year, he flew with her to Spain for several days. One day, after returning to the hotel room, Stacy found a bed scattered with roses and a diamond ring on a pillow.

"Oh my goodness," she said rushing forward to pick it up. "What is this?" She turned around to find Chance down on one knee.

"Stacy, will you marry me?"

She stared at him, at first not knowing what to say. She didn't need to get married again. Her head told her that her life was fine as it was. That they shouldn't change anything, but her heart shouted 'yes'. She nodded too moved to speak.

Chance scrambled to his feet. "Really?"

"Yes," she said sliding the ring on her finger.

He laughed. "I don't think I've been so nervous in my life, except when I first went on stage." He hugged her and her heart rejoiced but an uneasiness in her mind slowly grew, demanding answers she didn't want to know. Why hadn't she met his family yet? Where had she known him before? Why did he change the subject when she asked about his past? But she brushed those thoughts aside. With him Stacy felt happier than she'd ever known. She'd been given the second chance at the love life she'd hoped for. Being part of the Black Stockings Society had worked, she was successful, living life to the fullest with a man she loved. That was until one early spring day when she was forced to face what Chance had been hiding.

CHAPTER TWENTY-ONE

"Is Uncle Chance with you?" Tiffany asked in a hurried tone.

"No," Stacy said. She sat in her office. She knew Chance was probably on a set somewhere and likely out of reach. "What's wrong?"

"Idon'tknowwhattodo," Tiffany said, so quickly it sounded like gibberish. "He won't answer his phone and I can't get Uncle Leon either and--"

"Slow down," Stacy said keeping her voice calm. "Tell me what's wrong."

"Mom's acting strange and I'm scared," the little girl said near tears.

"Are you home right now?"

"Yes."

"I'll be right over."

She sent Chance a vague text that she'd gone to see Tiffany, but she didn't want to alarm him, then drove to her house. Stacy knocked and rang the doorbell. No one answered. She knocked again, then pounded on the door, her anxiety growing. "Tiffany? It's me, honey."

Tiffany swung open the door. "I'm sorry. I was in the bathroom and couldn't hear you."

"Don't be sorry," Stacy said entering the house. The scent of burnt food, old carpets and dank air filled the air. She found Maris sitting on the couch just staring at the blank TV screen.

"Hi, Maris. I'm sure you don't want to see me but--"

"I don't care," she said in a hollow tone.

"Are you okay?"

"I'm fine. I'm just sitting here listening to the fairies."

"She keeps saying that over and over again," Tiffany whispered.

"I think we need to call an ambulance."

Tiffany vehemently shook her head. "No, I'll get in trouble. They were so angry last time."

"Who?"

"Uncle Leon said I was to call him if anything happened with Mom, but I can't reach him or Uncle Chance."

"He can get angry at me," Stacy said quickly assessing the situation. "I'm glad you called me. Your mother needs to see a doctor."

"I don't need to see a doctor," Maris said, her words slightly slurred. "We've got a doctor in the family and that's all I need."

"Well, doctors work in hospitals, right? So maybe he's there."

Maris nodded, as if considering her words. "Yes, that's right. He works at a hospital." She stood. "I can't go like this. Let me go change. Look after the fairies, some follow me, but some like to stay behind."

"Of course," Stacy said then dialed 9 1 1 as Maris shuffled down the hall.

She was talking to the dispatcher when someone opened the front door with such force that the entire house shook. Moments later, Stacy heard a deep voice. "Where is she?" a man said barreling into the room. He stared at Stacy. He had Chance's good looks, but Marshall's eyes. Cold, calculating eyes. Stacy quickly brushed the thought aside. She hardly knew the man and she had no right to judge him, although his hard gaze made a shiver of fear course through her.

"I just called an ambulance," she said. "The dispatcher--"

"Cancel it."

"I can't. They're already on their way."

He snatched the phone from her. "I'm Dr. Paige. I've arrived on the scene. You don't need to send anyone. I'll handle the situation. Yes, I know, but I don't want to waste your time." He nodded then hung up. He glared at his niece. "I told you to wait for me."

She hunched her shoulders and rubbed her hands. "I didn't--"

"I'm the one who called," Stacy said, in no mood to see a child get into trouble for a decision she'd made.

"I don't care," he said. "Tiffany knows better."

"I think she may need--"

"Thank you for helping here. I can take over." He turned to his sister when she came back into the living room.

She clapped her hands and beamed. "You came! I was just going to see you."

"Yes, you need to rest now. Have you taken your medicine?"

"I'm listening to the fairies. They're all over the house now."

"Of course you are." He took her arm and led her away.

Stacy watched him go. She didn't like him, but he wasn't the one she was worried about. She looked at Tiffany, who hadn't moved. She softened her tone. "Your mother is going to be okay."

"Uncle Leon is going to be so angry."

"He's angry with me, not you. Have you had anything to eat yet?"

"No."

Stacy went into the kitchen and winced. It was filthy. Unwashed dishes, some recently broken, sat inside the fridge. She smelled the rotten food before she even saw it. She opened a cupboard and saw several roaches scurry past. She quickly closed it. She needed to get Tiffany some food, but knew the girl needed much more. Did Chance know his niece lived like this?

"I think we'll do take out, but first I have to call a friend." She dialed Laurice. "I really hate asking you to do this."

"What?"

"I need your help cleaning a place. I wouldn't ask if it wasn't important."

"Bonus pay?"

Stacy glanced around the kitchen at the enormous task at hand. Laurice had every right to refuse. "Triple."

"Give me the address."

She did then ordered pizza.

Leon came into the room and snatched her cell phone. "What are you doing?"

"Getting dinner," she said snatching the phone back. "Didn't your mother teach you any manners?"

"Who are you?"

"Tiffany, would you please go into the other room and wait for the pizza and my friend."

The girl nodded then left.

"Your friend's coming here?" Leon asked.

"Yes."

Leon folded his arms, pinning her with a dark gaze. "You still haven't told me who you are."

"I'm a friend of Tiffany's," she said, refusing to be intimidated. "And I don't think Tiffany should stay here."

"Why not?"

"There's rotten food in the fridge, there are cockroaches and--"

"So what? No one is going to take a child away from her mother because of some moldy food and insects. Sure, it's not the best environment, but kids grow up in a lot worse and who are you to judge anyway? I'm her Uncle and I'm here now so it's no longer your concern."

"Tiffany is scared."

"She's just worried about her mother, but she gets over it. Maris had a bad day, that's all."

"I think it's more than that."

He rested his hands on his hips and took an aggressive step forward. "I'm sorry, who the hell are you again?"

"A friend," Stacy said boldly meeting his gaze.

"Look, I don't want to be rude or anything but this is really none of your business. Thanks." He gestured to the door. "You can leave now."

Stacy kept his steady gaze, ready for a fight. "But I'm not going to."

He grabbed her arm in a vice-like grip. "Yes, you are."

Stacy only smiled.

The doorbell rang.

He swore. "Who the hell--"

"That's the pizza." She sent a pointed look at his hand. He sighed then released her. Stacy answered the door and paid the delivery carrier then called out in a bright tone, "Come on Tiffany, dinner's here," even though inside she felt cold. Leon reminded her too much of a predator. As she placed the pizza box on the coffee table in the living room, then set the pizza slices on the cleanest cracked plates she could find, she felt his gaze on her. An ugly, assessing gaze that made her skin crawl. She now understood why Chance hadn't invited her to any family dinners.

"Maris, is enough," he'd once said when she'd asked him.

Tiffany ate with gusto, but Stacy had little appetite and was relieved when Laurice finally arrived. Laurice and Leon shared a brief look before Leon dismissed her with a crude word and looked at Stacy stunned. "She's your friend?"

"Yes," she said. "Thanks for doing this. The kitchen is

where we need to start," she said pointing to where Laurice should go.

"Friend huh?" Leon said with a snort. "Did you pick her up while doing some research or something?"

Stacy spun around ready to reply, but Laurice gave her a light nudge. "Leave it alone. You've got to be careful," she said in a low voice before disappearing into the kitchen.

"What are you two planning to do?" Leon asked.

"Clean this place up," Stacy said, finding a broom in the hallway closet and briefly imagining shoving the handle up his backside.

"Don't move things. My sister is particular and I don't want her to get upset." His cell phone rang. "Hey, yes I'm with her now. Things are fine." He listened a few minutes then snorted. "Oh, so you think you're a doctor now because you play one on TV? I told you she's fine. Tiffany is eating with some woman she says is a *friend*."

Stacy walked into the kitchen where Laurice was stacking dishes. "If that man were a cockroach I'd gladly stomp him into the ground."

"Keep your voice down."

Stacy looked her surprised. It wasn't like Laurice to be timid. "Why?"

"I told you to be careful of him."

"I'm trying to be as nice as I can since he's Chance's brother."

Laurice swore.

Stacy laughed feeling the same. "I know. Every family has a jerk, right?"

"No." Laurice shook her head. "I mean...never mind. Let's just clean up this dump and get out of here."

～

THERE WERE three things Chance didn't expect to see when he went to his sister's house. One, Stacy's car still there, two, to step inside and see how clean and orderly everything looked and lastly, to see his family sitting in the living room waiting for him. His sister, resting her head on his mother's shoulder, his brother and Gran.

"It's about time you got here," Leon said.

Chance glanced around the room with a sense of dread. "Where's Stacy?"

"Sleeping with Tiffany, after cleaning this place like a crazy woman," Leon replied. He blocked his way. "But before you wake her up, we need to talk."

"About what?"

"About you dragging other people into private family matters."

"I didn't."

"Then how did Tiffany get her number?"

"She had it in case of emergencies," Chance said.

"Maris just had a bad spell. Tiffany knows better than that. You've been telling her things haven't you?"

"No, Tiffany is just older and knows when something's not right. We can't keep pretending—"

"Do you really want the truth about this to get out?"

"No, but she needs--"

"She's fine. She doesn't need to see another doctor." His brother shook his head. "You don't even know how much trouble you've caused. She's seen the house and she could report her."

"She won't," Chance said.

"This conversation is fruitless. Maris just had a bad spell. She's fine and so is Tiffany. She's doing well in school and she's happy. "

"Let's just consider giving Maris some time. I'll hire a live in nurse so that Tiffany can stay with Mom."

"I have enough energy to take care of Gran," Althea said. "I don't want anybody else."

"You can move into a bigger space."

"I like where I am."

"Why not have Tiffany stay with us a few days?" Gran said.

Althea sent her mother a look. "Mom, I'm not having it and that's final. Chance come here." He followed her into the kitchen. "Are you really trying to rip this family apart?" she asked.

"You know I'm not."

"'Threatening your sister with Child Protective Services, telling your brother that his diagnosis is wrong, and telling me that I should move to suit a child? Who do you think you are? Do you know why you're here? Do you know why you're on some big TV show and making money? Because of me. Because I had to give up everything to take care of you three. I had a life before you and now you're trying to tear apart everything I've had to sacrifice for."

"I'm trying to make things easier."

"Easier? Even when you were a kid you always acted like you knew more than me. No more. Do you know why you're here? Because when your father died, and our mother was sick with cancer, she called me and pleaded with me to take care of you. I was only nineteen and all of a sudden I had three kids under five to look after. Aunty helped, but it was still a struggle. I took you three out of a hovel in the East End of London and brought you all here. The life I'd wanted for myself was gone. But did I complain? No. I let you call me Mom and call Aunty, Gran. I made a family for you.

"Did I say anything when you didn't go to college as we'd all hoped? No. Did I say anything about that other choice you made? The one we're all dealing with right now."

"No," Chance said steeling himself against the words that were always thrown at him at moments like this. Just when he felt he could feel part of a real family, she reminded him that it was only an illusion of one. That he was her charity case half-brother. That he owed all of his success to her. To her, he was never grateful enough. Never beholden enough. She'd never understand how her words hurt him. How much he did love her. That she was the only mother he'd ever known, that he wanted to buy her a house, or something to show his gratitude. But she preferred to stay as she was.

"That's right. You owe me respect and that means you don't tell me what to do. Tiffany is fine. A cockroach or two never killed anyone. It will give her character. She's too soft anyway. She needs some strength. You're a man. I know how a girl should be raised. I'll look after your sister as I always have." Her eyes glistened with tears and her mouth turned hard. "My sacrifice won't be for nothing. Are we clear?"

He nodded then turned away.

"You know I love you, right?"

He nodded.

"Then give me a kiss."

Chance briefly squeezed his eyes shut then turned and kissed her cheek.

"Thank you," she said giving him a quick pat on the back before she left.

He stayed in the kitchen and gripped his hands into fists. He couldn't believe Stacy had been pulled into this mess.

"What are you waiting for?" His grandmother said behind him. "You might as well go and wake her up. I'd like to meet her."

"You can meet her another day."

She sighed. "Fine, if you don't want me to meet her. Who knows how many days I have left. You young people always think about tomorrow, but a woman of my age only has today. The present is the only moment I can treasure, the only time I can--"

"All right," he said resigned. "I'll go get her."

~

HE COULDN'T PROTECT HER. He couldn't protect either of them. Chance stood at the foot of Tiffany's bed and watched them sleep. He wanted to hug Tiffany and tell her how sorry he was. Every day he wondered if he'd made the right choice. Recently, he didn't believe so. He shifted his gaze to Stacy. He wanted to marry her more than he could ever explain. He wanted her softness to combat his mother's hard words. He wanted her comfort, her understanding, her acceptance. With her, he had a place where he belonged.

He gently shook Stacy awake then gestured for her to follow him.

"Thanks for staying with her," he said when they were alone in the hallway. He closed the door behind him.

"I had to. She seemed so scared."

"We can go now. She'll be fine and--"

"Chance, things are really bad here."

He sighed. "I know. My family's discussing our options."

"What options?"

He wished she hadn't asked him, he hated dragging her into the middle of a family crisis, but he knew she deserved the truth. "My sister has always had troubles. Even as a little boy, I remember her disappearing for weeks, but I never knew why. It wasn't until I was older that I learned about the different places they'd placed her because of her mental health issues. She'd seemed stable for a time, but she's recently gotten worse. I think she should get special care, but my brother thinks we can handle things." He was silent a moment. "You know, it's funny. On TV I'm seen as the good guy who has bad things happen to him, but in real life, I'm the bad guy. I'm the guy who wants to take a daughter away from her mother. To remove her from the only home she's ever known. But it's not like that. If I could trust my sister, I wouldn't even consider it. But I'm worried about Tiffany. I want more for her. But a mother's love trumps an Uncle's love, right? And she needs a woman and I know there are things I can't give her, but I think she deserves to feel safe. But my mother and brother think I should leave things alone and they act like I'm the bad guy."

"But you're not."

He looked at her surprised. "You--you understand?"

"Your brother and I almost came to blows when I first saw what your sister and niece are living in. It's not just the filth. It's not about a bare fridge. It's about how Tiffany feels. I had a good friend whose parents never had a lot. Sometimes flies got into the house and there were fleas everywhere, but there was also love and a sense of safety. Her parents did their best. That's not the situation here. It's clear your sister can't manage and provide a place of safety and Tiffany is suffering--" She stopped when Chance started to smile. "What?"

"You really understand." He looked down at her relieved. "Do you know how good this feels? This is the first time I can talk about this. Nobody else knows. I keep it to myself. I don't want CPS to swoop in, but it's getting worse, not better, and no one in my family will listen to me. My brother is the last word because he's the doctor. But doctors can be wrong. I don't know why he won't look into other options. I've offered to pay for a nanny so that Tiffany can stay with my mom or have live in help for Gran. But he thinks our sister needs to have her independence. He's afraid a major change will undermine her progress." He swore. "They're all waiting in the other room to pounce on you. Just nod and then we'll leave."

"I don't care what they have to say. I--"

"I know you want to do more. So do I, but--"

"She's not your child."

"That's just the problem. She's not really Maris's child either."

Stacy's eyes widened. "She's yours?"

Chance heaved a heavy sigh and shook his head. "No, I stole her."

CHAPTER TWENTY-TWO

Stacy started to laugh, but the look on his face stopped her. "You're serious?"

He nodded. "I honestly don't know what I was thinking at the time. It happened early in my career. I was staying in a nasty basement apartment in Queens, going on auditions and getting nowhere. I was coming home late one night when I overheard a woman talking to a young girl about dumping something in the Hudson. I didn't pay much attention until I caught what she was talking about. I really couldn't believe what I was hearing. They were talking about a baby. The girl started to walk down towards the river when her mother called her back inside leaving the baby alone in the stroller.

Chance took a deep breath and briefly covered his eyes. "That's when I snatched her. I thought of taking her to a hospital, but I wasn't sure I could get away with them not asking me any questions. So I called my mother. I thought she could tell me of a children's home or somewhere. She told me to bring the baby home. When I arrived, she said that a baby was just what Maris needed. She had married, but hadn't been able to conceive and after her husband left her she went into a deep depression. The baby made the difference. She instantly took to the child so we decided to keep her. My sister was doing better then and I had nothing to offer a child. We faked some papers and made it legal."

"How?"

Chance lifted a brow. "Do you really want to know?"

"No. Go on."

"After a couple of years she started drinking and her health deteriorated. By then it was too late. My brother threatened to expose me. Just think of how it would look if people discover that I'm not only a baby snatcher, but we fabricated a child's life. And I don't want Tiffany exposed to the ugliness people like to read about. If I wasn't who I am now, I would fight for her, but I don't want her used to sell papers and online views." He paused. "Are you laughing at me?"

"I'm sorry, I don't mean to, I just can't get over the fact that you stole a baby. I never would have guessed."

"Quiet, do you want them to hear us?"

Stacy covered her mouth and shook her head.

"I told you, it's not something I'm proud of." He rubbed the back of his neck. "I shouldn't have told you."

Stacy took his hand. "I'm glad you did. It's just a bigger problem than I thought. Does Tiffany know?"

Chance widened his eyes. "Do you think I'd tell her a story like that?"

"What does she think?"

"She knows she's adopted. But Maris won't give up custody. It will be a fight to get her to relinquish her rights. And a court case could destroy her."

Stacy rested her head on his shoulder and groaned. "The last thing I want is to be involved in another court case."

"I know."

"But I think I know someone I can talk to."

"You'll help me?"

Stacy looked at him surprised. "Of course I'll help you."

"You don't know what's at stake. *Courting Danger* has not been released yet and even when it is, if my reputation is ruined it may--"

"I know how things work. We're going to be strategic and figure out something."

Leon came into the hallway. "I was wondering what was taking you two so long."

"We're talking," Chance said.

"Mom needs you."

"Fine."

"I'll be all right," Stacy said.

Chance nodded then left her. Stacy went into the kitchen to put on some tea. Leon followed her and sat down.

"I guess you both belong to the land of make believe," he said. "Making money while the rest of us do real work."

"Were you weaned too early or something?"

"What?"

"I've never heard such a big baby in my whole life."

"Excuse me?"

"This is the way the world works. You need us and we need you. The head and the heart. It's all one."

"My work matters more."

"Yes, and what do people do after surgery? How best do they heal? By watching a funny movie, or reading a book, or looking at a painting, or talking with friends?"

"People worship people who don't matter. Why do we worship someone just because they're famous?"

"Not everyone does," Stacy said not surprised by the jealousy she heard in Leon's tone. She'd heard the same in Marshall's voice. "It only seems that way. There are actors and writers you've never heard of but millions of others have. There are doctors and scientists I don't know about but millions of lives have been affected by them. Does it matter who's popular as long as you live with joy? As long as you make your life matter? I don't write so that people know me, and most don't, but I make a lot of money entertaining people and making them happy. Your brother does the same. But I'm assuming that's not the same with you. You probably didn't become a doctor because you had a passion for it. You did it for status and prestige and that's why it irks you that your brother gets what you think you should. Because, if you truly loved your work, nothing else would matter."

He stood and closed the distance between them. "You don't know anything about me."

"I'm right, aren't I? You hate your schedule. You hate your patients. You hate your career and if you could do it all over again you'd chose something else. What you hate the most is that you feel stuck because you feel that should be happy because people are impressed by what you do, but it's not enough. You sacrificed so much and you're still not happy. Am I close?"

Leon's eyes hardened. "Are you in the market to make my brother husband number two?"

"My relationship with your brother has nothing to do with you."

"That's where you're wrong. Look, you may have my brother by the balls, but I've got him where it counts." He tapped his chest. "Right here, and there's nothing you can do about it. You'll never last without me. If I want you to disappear, you'll be gone. You're a sad, pathetic bitter divorcee and you have nothing to say considering you hang out with whores," he said grabbing her butt and squeezing it hard.

"Take your hand off me," she said in a cool, clipped tone.

"You think I don't know who that woman was you brought here, bitch?"

Stacy looked into his eyes and saw Marshall's gaze again and knew how dangerous Leon was. But this time she didn't care. She saw red and launched at him like a wildcat. She scratched his face, and kicked him. She couldn't remember much of the rest, just that moments later someone was pulling her away. She saw three other faces staring at her in shock. She only recognized Maris.

"What are you doing?" Chance said, grabbing her around the waist.

"She just came at me," Leon said in a shaky voice, grabbing the side of his face where Stacy had struck him. "What the hell is wrong with her?"

Chance glared at her. "Have you lost your mind? You

know how I feel about violence. After what I shared with you. What our father put us through, how could you do this in my sister's house?"

"But he--"

"I don't care. There's no excuse for violence. Ever. I don't care if you break things, smash things, spit on things, but you touch another human being in anger and you've gone too far."

Stacy saw Leon grin and knew she couldn't let him win. "Chance, I--"

"I don't want to hear it. Apologize now."

She pulled away from him. "No."

He stared at her for a moment, unsure. "What do you mean 'no'?"

"I will not apologize to him. Ever."

"Take a deep breath. I understand you're angry, but you're going to apologize then we'll get to the bottom of things."

"No."

"Do you see those scratch marks on my brother's face? Do you want me to tell you about the time our stepfather used a fork to peel away my skin when I did something wrong?"

Stacy looked down at her hands, she saw her engagement ring smeared with his brother's blood. She knew how things looked. She knew that, in an instant, Chance was no longer the man she loved, but judge and jury who'd just convicted her--finding her guilty. She now understood why he hadn't introduced her to his family. He didn't love her enough. "I am not your stepfather," she said in a tired, hollow voice, all fight gone.

"I know that, but what I'm saying is that anger must always be controlled. It's dangerous otherwise."

"You're right," she said, twisting off her ring.

Chance covered her hand before she could pull the ring off completely. "What are you doing?"

"Letting him win."

"Stacy, I don't know what happened, but I'm sure it was all a misunderstanding." His hand closed around hers and he softened his tone. "My brother would never hurt a woman. He can be coarse and foul I know, but he'd never touch one. We both made a promise. Even now he helps battered women for free."

Tears shone in her eyes. "I'm not going to apologize."

Chance's voice dropped to a whisper, cracking with pain. "Just do it for me. We can talk about--"

"No, there's nothing more to say." She set the engagement ring on the counter, pushed past him, then raced out of the house and jumped into her car. She drove a few blocks away then parked her car and just screamed. She screamed until her voice was hoarse. She screamed while hot tears spilled down her cheeks. She screamed her rage. She screamed her pain. She screamed her sorrow. Why did she always have to lose? Why couldn't Chance have just listened to her? Why couldn't he have loved her enough to have given her the benefit of the doubt? She just wanted to be heard. She wanted to be believed. She had risked so much for him and he'd left her empty and she had no Julia to run to. She was truly alone and she had no one to blame but herself.

∾

"I'M REALLY SORRY ABOUT THAT," Leon said once they were alone.

Chance nodded. "I know."

Leon's gaze dropped to the ring left sitting on the counter. "So what's that about?"

Chance snatched the ring up and shoved it in his pocket. Stacy was gone. She'd really left him, leaving their future behind. "A mistake."

Tiffany came into the kitchen rubbing her eyes. "Did Aunt Stacy leave?"

He nodded, unable to speak, the room suddenly feeling smaller, the air thin.

"Go back to bed," Leon said.

Tiffany didn't move. She lightly touched Chance's hand. "Are you okay?"

Chance nodded again, keenly aware of how quickly his chest rose and fell. He couldn't afford a panic attack now. He had to stay strong for her.

"Go to bed," Leon said again, this time his tone held a level of command. After she'd gone, he looked at Chance with concern. "Are you sure you're all right?"

"I'm fine," he wheezed, reminding himself of the kid who'd suffered childhood asthma and disappeared into the movies when his stepfather scared him. He watched his brother leave the kitchen then fell into a chair. This was the man Stacy didn't want to marry. She only wanted Chance Jamison--the successful actor and producer. The man who took her to plays and wined and dined her. Not Terrell Paige--the man with a complicated family life, a man who suffered major panic attacks. A man who abhorred violence. Chance wouldn't care. Chance was perfect, easy-going, understanding, unafraid. He'd thought his dream had finally come true, that he wouldn't be lonely anymore. But he'd been wrong.

~

IN THE OTHER ROOM, Leon had to hide a smile.

"What trouble have you been making?" his Gran said with a knowing look.

Leon wiped the smile from his face. "Nothing. I didn't do anything." He kissed her on the cheek. "I'd better get going," he said then left. Getting rid of Stacy had been easier than he'd thought. *Who's the great one now, bro?* He may have the career and the fans, but now his love life was in the toilet. Exactly where it should be. Stacy learned that she couldn't match him either. That she may be smart, but not as smart as he was. She was just a woman and he knew how to handle them. He'd tried to be soft, but the ones he liked wanted it rough. His brother would soon learn the truth too. That women couldn't be trusted and only fools gave their hearts away. Tonight he'd seen that their love was as fake as the crap they created. They got a real dose of reality and couldn't handle it. Now they would know how the rest of the world felt. How it felt to be a real person with a job. He could still see Chance's face--horrified, shocked, hurt. He should get an Emmy for that role. He couldn't smile now. He couldn't be the star of the show. But most of all, he couldn't outshine him.

CHAPTER TWENTY-THREE

STACY WALKED into the living room feeling like a wrung-out dishrag. Houdini greeted her and she fell to her knees and hugged him, pressing her cheek against his soft fur. "You're the only one who's stayed by my side." She looked at him and he licked her face, his tail wagging.

Laurice came up to her and said, "You have a visitor. But first I think there's something you should know about--"

"Who's here?" Stacy cut in. She glanced at her watch. "It's nearly ten."

"She told me you were expecting her."

"I'm not expecting anybody--"

Rania came around the corner. "That's too bad because we need to talk."

"Not now. I have a lot of things I have to do. We can talk later." She went into her bedroom.

"I think you should listen to what Laurice has to say," Rania said, standing in the doorway.

"I can listen to it later. Right now I just need some time alone."

"But I think it might help--"

Stacy pounded the bed. "I don't care! Do you hear me? I don't care. I don't want to listen, I don't want to talk. I just want to be left alone."

"Have you forgotten the oath?" Rania said after a few moments.

"I know it by heart."

"Then why are you settling?"

"I'm not settling. The Black--" She lowered her voice when Rania gave her a look of sensor and realized she feared Laurice could overhear. "I mean this society has given me all that I wanted. I'm the one who screwed up."

"How?"

"I lost my temper when I shouldn't have."

"So just apologize."

"I can't."

"So you're settling. You're settling for what you can get instead of going out and fighting for what you want. If you truly loved Chance, you'd talk to him. You'd both figure this out together."

"I guess I don't really love him then, huh? Which is great, since he certainly doesn't love me."

"How do you know that?"

"What are you even doing here? How did you know...look can we do this another time?"

"You're avoiding the question."

"If you'd seen the look on Chance's face you'd know."

"Did you see him clearly or did you see him through eyes of anger?"

Stacy clenched her fist remembering Chance's dark look when he asked her to apologize. "I saw him clearly for the first time."

Rania nodded. "Then you're right. You don't love him and you don't love yourself, either."

"Now wait a minute. I've done everything this club has asked of me. I've worn the stockings and felt better than I ever have. I've gotten over my divorce, I'm writing again and I'm successful. That's a woman who loves herself."

"It's an illusion of one."

"I don't need a man to make me happy."

"I never said that."

"It's implied."

"No, I'm saying you're settling because you don't think you're worthy of having it all. Why can't you strive to have a great career and someone to share it with? You think that you have to be alone to be a successful woman. You've given yourself only one option."

"He's the one who *left* me. He didn't stand up for me. He took his brother's side. He asked me to apologize."

"And you wouldn't?"

"No."

"Why not?"

Stacy felt tears build and this time she let them fall. "Because I'm tired of apologizing. I'm tired of apologizing for being too successful or not successful enough, for being too ambitious, too driven, too aggressive. I'm tired of being the one who no one believes, no one sides with. I thought he was different, but he's like all the rest. He got what he wanted and left me high and dry. I wonder how long it will take him to find my replacement."

Rania sat on the bed. "Tell me exactly what happened."

"I thought you already knew."

Rania shrugged and stood. "You seemed like you wanted someone to hear your side so I was giving you the opportunity, but if you don't want to--"

"It happened like this..." Stacy said then told Rania about the entire day ending with her storming out of Maris's place. "And that's it."

Rania sighed. "You're right. You did screw up."

"I did?"

"Yes. He wasn't asking you to apologize. He was asking you to say 'I love you'."

"What?"

"You said that his stepfather was abusive?"

"Yes."

"Ever consider that what he saw you do may have not made him angry, but frightened him instead? Flip it around. How would you feel if you invited Chance over here and he did something violent to Laurice."

"That's different."

"Why? Because you're a woman? Why couldn't you have just apologized not to Leon, but to him. That's all he needed."

"But he already knows I love him. I said I would marry him."

Rania glanced down at Stacy's hand. "So where's the ring?"

"I gave it back."

Rania nodded. "So you fight with his brother, refuse to apologize, then return his ring and he's supposed to know that you love him? You're all mixed up."

She'd never thought of it that way. She'd never taken the time to see things from Chance's perspective. It had been a highly emotional time, but she'd only seen anger not fear. She sunk down onto the bed. "You're right."

"Talk to Chance." Rania moved in close and held her hand.

"No, I can't go back to him. I've hurt him too much. I keep comparing him to Marshall, even when I don't mean to. I can't hurt him again. I won't."

"Stacy--"

"You were right. I did get a new love life and I don't regret it, it just didn't last as long as I'd hoped. I want Chance to find someone who doesn't hurt or frighten him or..." She swallowed.

"Stacy, that woman is you."

She smiled with sadness. "I used to think so."

"You haven't worn your fourth pair of stockings yet."

"I know. I was supposed to wear them to a special occasion. I was waiting for my wedding day."

"Wear them to the next rehearsal at the theatre."

"But that's not special."

"Isn't it? Remember when getting a play produced was just a dream? Don't ever become so jaded that even small moments mean nothing. Wear the stockings. That's an order."

Laurice knew it wasn't her place, but she felt like she had to do something. She wanted to stop Stacy from making a big mistake. Since Stacy wouldn't listen to her, she'd make Chance. She saw him go into his apartment building. She called after him, but he didn't hear her. She rushed up to him and grabbed his arm. "I've gotta talk to you."

He turned and she froze. He wasn't Chance, but Leon.

"You're out of your neighborhood," Leon said with a cold stare.

Laurice quickly released him and turned.

He grabbed her arm and spun her around. "What do you want to see my brother for?"

"No reason."

"Running errands for your lady?"

"It was just about the script. He'll find out later."

"Tell me and I'll pass the information on."

"No, it's private."

He pushed his face close up to hers. "Did you come here for another reason and don't want anyone to know?"

Laurice stared back at him, used to the ugly look in his eyes. He only saw women in one way. "I'm going now."

"You didn't answer my question," he said then glanced up and his expression changed. He quickly released her.

A second later she discovered why. "Hey, what are you doing here?" Chance asked, coming up behind her.

Laurice rubbed her sore arm. She couldn't say anything while Leon was still around. She didn't want to lose this opportunity, but she couldn't take such a risk either. "You're busy. I'll come back later."

"Has something happened to Stacy?"

She sent a significant glance to Leon. "It's private."

"I'm sure it is," Leon said in a nasty tone.

Chance ignored him. "Come on, I feel like getting a drink."

"That sounds like a good idea," Leon said.

"You're not invited so don't even think about following us."

"But I came to talk to you."

"I'll talk to you later." Chance took Laurice's arm and led her away.

Laurice glanced back at Leon, determined that one day she'd get him back for what he did to Rockett.

~

A FEW MINUTES later the two sat in a restaurant. Chance rubbed his hands on his jeans feeling more eager than he wanted to. What did Laurice have to say? Why had Stacy sent her? Was she willing to apologize?

"I'll just get straight to the point. You have to be careful of your brother."

"What?" Chance said feeling his heart drop to his knees. *His brother?* Nearly every one warned him about his conniving TV brother, but why was she talking about his show right now?

"He's dangerous."

Chance sat back in his chair annoyed, but kept his voice polite. Maybe since he'd used her for the consulting job she thought she was doing him a favor. Diehard fans tended to confuse truth with reality. "Everyone knows that? It's how the show's written."

Laurice shook her head. "No, I'm not talking about the show. I'm talking about Leon."

He paused. "My brother and I sometimes have our differences, but he's good to me."

"Fine, if that's all that matters."

"What do you mean? What did Stacy say?"

"You're not going to believe me." She stood. "I shouldn't have come."

He touched her hand and gently pulled her back down. "Did my brother do something to her?"

"I don't know. She wouldn't talk to me, I just know your brother. He's got a reputation with the ladies."

"I know that."

Laurice shook her head amused. "I mean the ladies on the street. He's known as the Hands. He's into S and M, which is fine but he takes it to another level. He left two girls nearly dead. One was a good friend of mine named Rockett. I don't know what happened at your house but if your brother is in anyway involved, you don't know the full story. That's all I want to say."

"Did they tell the police?"

Laurice looked at him, deadpan. "That's a joke, right?"

"What about their pimps? Don't they offer protection?"

"Pimps don't mess with one of their own."

Chance stared at her in utter disbelief. "What?"

"He's in with them. He gives them the dope they

need. He keeps his hands clean enough and it was only luck that I saw him. He doesn't do business in the city."

Chance shook his head. "I'm sorry, but you're wrong. You must have my brother confused with someone else. He's in a long term relationship and he respects women."

"I know who he is." Laurice lifted up her shirt sleeve and showed him the bruise Leon had left.

"My brother did that?"

"Just before you saw us and he was being nice."

"But it doesn't make sense. I've never seen Leon hurt anyone. He became a doctor to heal and help people."

Laurice stood. "That's right. I'm just an ex-hooker. You don't have to believe me."

"Sit down, I'm not saying that. I mean...tell me what Stacy said."

"I told you, she didn't say anything," Laurice said taking her seat. "What did she tell you?"

Nothing. I didn't give her a chance to explain. He silently swore. Could his brother have hurt her too? Why? Had he really gotten everything all wrong? His brother was family. This wasn't some TV melodrama. They looked out for each other. What could his brother have against Stacy? He didn't even know her, he'd only met her once. "Thanks," he said.

Laurice's liquid brown gaze turned sour. "You don't believe me."

Chance sighed, feeling frustrated and confused. "Why are you telling me this?"

"In case you get another girlfriend. You need to look out for her. You did me one turn and I thought I'd return the favor."

"Thanks."

She folded her arms and sneered. "You still don't believe me."

"It doesn't matter what I believe. Stacy and I are through."

"Because of Leon?"

"I know my brother a lot better than I know Stacy. My brother wouldn't lie to me. I'm sorry about your friend but, maybe some S&M got out of hand."

Laurice stared at him for a long moment then shook her head in disgust. "I thought I could trust you. I thought you were different."

Chance stood. "Yea, well don't make that mistake again."

Laurice swore. "I was wrong. Julia was right about you."

~

JULIA WAS RIGHT ABOUT YOU. The words stung but he didn't care. He knew his little brother. He knew what they'd both gone through. Two days later Chance rode the elevator to Tyson's office, wishing he could erase the sight of Stacy pulling off his ring. He needed to keep busy. He knew that would be the cure. He walked into the office and grinned at the receptionist then walked into Tyson's office after knocking. He smiled at his friend then his smile froze when he saw who was with him.

CHAPTER TWENTY-FOUR

HE SAW a distinguished looking man with spiky white hair, a trimmed goatee that was still brown and laughing hazel eyes. Heisman. Thomas Heisman his idol, the film-maker he'd always wanted to meet, sitting in Tyson's office. The older man stood up and held out his hand. Chance shook it, feeling ten years old again. Heisman was shaking his hand.

"Sorry for not making an appointment, but I have to get on a plane in a few hours and wanted to drop by. I've seen some of your work and wondered if you'd ever thought of collaborating?"

This wasn't happening. He was dreaming.

"Chance?" Tyson said.

Chance blinked and turned to his friend, feeling as if everything were happening in slow motion. "What?"

Heisman laughed. "No, pressure. I know your schedule is busy--"

It was real. Heisman was really talking to him. "No,"

Chance said quickly. "I mean yes...uh...I'd love to work with you on something."

"Send some projects my way."

"But we can't afford you."

He grinned. "Stacy told me you're a great negotiator. I'm sure we can work out something."

"Stacy?" he said, grabbing onto her name as if it were a life raft. "You spoke to Stacy?"

"Yes, about two days ago."

"Stacy Price knows you?" he said just to make sure.

"Yes, we'd worked together before. She couldn't say enough about you." He glanced at his watch. "I'd better get going." He handed him his business card. "I know it's old school, but I still use the phone." He nodded then left.

Tyson took the card from Chance and stared at it in awe. "What the hell just happened?"

"I don't know." Heisman had spoken to Stacy two days ago? But they'd broken up by then. She'd given him back his ring and then made one of his childhood dreams come true? It didn't make sense. But then again it did. This was the Stacy he knew. The woman with a generous heart, who always thought of others. Then why had she attacked his brother? His brother said he hadn't insulted her, Laurice hinted at something more. Had his brother lied? Could his little brother really be the man Laurice talked about? He had to uncover the truth.

∾

"He's even better looking in person," Leon overheard a nurse say as he made his way to his office.

Before he could ask who, the receptionist said, "Your brother's here."

Leon plastered on a smile while he inwardly groaned. He hated when his brother came to visit his place of work.

"I'm busy," Leon said when he found Chance sitting in his office. It had been a week since he'd last seen him taking that whore Laurice out for a drink. He wished he'd taken a picture with his phone. Chance Jamison with a hooker would have made great press. "What do you want?" he asked taking a seat behind his desk.

"Why did you lie to me?"

"What are you talking about?"

"I'm talking about you and Stacy. You said she came at you for no reason."

Leon gestured to their surroundings. "Does this look like some studio set? I've got work to do." He stood. "I don't have time for this."

"Sit down little brother," Chance said in a cool tone.

"Why?"

"Because I'm asking you nicely."

Leon swallowed, suddenly feeling trapped. What did his brother know? Was he bluffing? Had Stacy gotten to him? "I didn't lie to you."

Chance nodded. "Okay, fine. Let's forget about Stacy. I have two ladies ready to charge you with assault."

Leon started to laugh. "Ladies? Have you been smoking something?"

"So you know who I'm talking about?"

"I know *what* you're talking about. A couple of hookers who want more dough."

"They seemed credible to me."

"It won't work."

"Court isn't much fun. Even if you win, your reputation will never be the same."

"How about yours? You think what happens to me won't affect you?"

Chance shrugged. "Not really."

"You're a criminal and I can reveal that."

Chance nodded unfazed. "That's right you fight dirty. Just like Althea's husband did, but I expected more. Tell me why? Why do you beat up women? Can't you take on a man?"

Leon surged towards his brother and pointed at him. "I can take you down."

Chance remained seated and kept his voice low. "Look at me little brother. Do you really think I hate violence because I'm scared? Do you think you frighten me in any way?" He stood and moved in close, facing him. He looked down at his fist. "You think I don't know my own strength?" He lifted his gaze. "If he hadn't died I would have killed him to protect you and Maris."

Leon stared back at his brother with anger, then a fissure of fear when he didn't see his brother's usual calm gaze but a seething rage. An expression he'd never seen on Chance's face before. But he'd seen that look in a man whose anger *had* terrified him. "You abandoned us instead."

"What?"

"After that bastard died, you left me behind to be everything Mom wanted you to be. I had to become the straight A student and doctor, while you were free."

"You didn't have to."

Leon pounded the desk. "I had no choice! You knew she didn't want us and I had to be the one to make up for it. I had to hear about how much she wanted to be a singer and that she'd had to give it all up. I had to hear how much you'd disappointed her, throwing all her struggles in her face. So I had to be the one she could brag about. So she could tell people that she raised a doctor. But I still ended up in your shadow."

"My shadow? Mom's never let me forget how much she sacrificed for us. But for the first time I realized how much her seething anger has poisoned us. My God, when you're hurting those women you're hurting her aren't you?"

"Don't tell me you've never thought of hurting her," Leon said in a dark, probing tone. "The way she talks to you. She's not our real mother."

"She's the only mother we've ever known."

"And she's hated every day of it. I'll never trust a woman."

Chance tapped the desk. "It stops now. The anger, the resentment. You're letting it destroy you, like it has her. It's time to let go of the past and heal."

~

MAGIC. That's what the theatre made her think of. It was home. Stacy stared at the now empty stage, the day's rehearsal was over. Her stockings had been a great conversation starter. She had decided to wear the floral stockings with a short black skirt and flat ballerina slippers. She'd turned heads and felt beautiful. It had been over a year since she'd been an angry divorcee. Now, she looked forward to the future.

Stacy picked up her bag and headed to the exit, but stopped when she saw a man sitting in the back row with his feet up on the chair in front of him, his hat low on his head. She paused surprised. She hadn't expected anyone else to be there. When he pushed his hat back and she saw his eyes her throat went dry. She felt as if the past and the present collided into one moment. She stared at him and suddenly remembered. Chance--but he wasn't the Chance from now and his name hadn't been Chance then. She saw another face--a younger version of him. A little heavier, wearing dark rimmed glasses and a shy grin. He didn't stand out like many of the other actors--especially Marshall--but he had a determination. "He'll end up being a character actor," she remembered one instructor saying.

Stacy stumbled forward a few steps then fell to her knees, remembering his words "The moment you remember me, you'll remember the woman you used to be." A raw and primitive sadness gripped her as she remembered an intensive Improv class one Indian summer more than ten years ago, and a quiet guy who froze on stage in front of a full crowd. She remembered Marshall snickering at him, but she'd felt mortified on his behalf. She remembered being his Improv partner the rest of the week, and coming up with different stage names he could use as a professional actor. She remembered letting him read and critique a script she'd been working on. Sharing her dreams with him and listening to his own. She remembered the passion, the enthusiasm with which she'd thrown herself into life. The drive with which she'd faced the future.

And as hot tears of loss gave way to regret she even remembered him saying on their last day of class, "Please don't forget me. I'm going to be a big success. Just you wait and see. One day I'll act in one of your plays." But she'd lost touch and she had forgotten him, only briefly allowing herself to remember him as initials T.P. in her imaginary diary. A life raft for her sinking dreams until she'd buried them completely. But he had come back into her life and given her hope again.

Chance ran towards her, knelt down and gathered her in his arms. "Stacy, what's wrong?"

Stacy squeezed her eyes shut and rested her head against his shoulder. This time the tears that escaped were of joy. She'd already fallen in love with him before, but now she felt as if she were falling in love all over again. Her heart feeling as if it would burst. "I remember you."

He stiffen. "What?"

Stacy drew back and stared at him, wiping away tears. "I remember you, Terrell Paige," she said, pronouncing his name with more feeling than she ever had knowing what it meant to her. She seized the front of his shirt, as if he were an aberration she was afraid would disappear. "I remember you!" she said again then hugged him. For one tense moment she felt him stiffen and wondered if she'd done something wrong, but before she could pull away, his arms circled around her and he held her tight. "I can't believe it's you," she said. Her fake diary had been the one place she hadn't looked when trying to remember him. She laughed.

Chance drew back and looked down at her. "What's so funny?"

"I've been thinking about you longer than I thought. Dreaming of you."

His brows shot up, his eyes bright with delight. "Of me?"

"Yes." She cupped his face. "I wrote about all the wonderful things we'd do together in a diary I made up. I never imagined they'd come true."

Chance gazed at her brown eyes, shining with both sadness and pleasure, before he turned away. "I'm sorry about my brother. He'll never touch you again."

She touched his chin, forcing him to face her. "And I'm sorry I gave you back my ring." She bit her lip. "Is there any way I can get it back?"

Chance pulled out the ring from his jeans pocket and slid it on her finger. He kept his gaze lowered and said, "I met Heisman."

"And did it go well?"

His eyes met and clung to hers. "I acted like a babbling idiot, but other than that it was perfect." He caressed the side of her face and his voice deepened into huskiness. "Just like this moment. One I've dreamt about for years." He bent down and kissed her, then whispered against her lips. "How would you write the ending of our story?"

Stacy threw her arms around his neck and gazed up at him with a happiness that made her heart dance. "What ending? Our story is just beginning..."

EPILOGUE

Two years later

THE TRADITIONAL PAIGE SUNDAY dinner gave way to movie night at the Jamison home. Tiffany, Gran and Althea sat in the large theatre room of Chance and Stacy's Long Island home. Tiffany now lived with them, as did Gran and her caretaker, who lived in the separate guest house, giving Althea the freedom to travel and live the life she'd always wanted. Maris now lived in a private rehabilitation facility where she was able to work on her addictions and mental health issues. Leon decided to quit being a physician and moved to a remote village in Zambia to help build wells. Laurice no longer worked for Stacy, but they remained close. After acting in a few movies and writing a book about her colorful life and a book of short stories which won two local literary prizes,

Lightning Source UK Ltd.
Milton Keynes UK
UKHW010630231021
392715UK00001B/63

9 781949 764529